The
Circus
Escape

Also by Thomas L. Tedrow

The Younguns/Book Three

The
Circus
Escape

❖

Thomas L. Tedrow

THOMAS NELSON PUBLISHERS
Nashville • Atlanta • London • Vancouver

To my family. Yesterday, today, forever.

Contents

The
Circus
Escape

Werewolf Boy

❖

Mansfield, Missouri
Summer 1908

It was a horrible thing being covered with hair. Even his eyelids. The only parts of his face spared the horrible affliction were his lips, which stood out firm, moist, and pink, and his eyes—his haunting, intelligent, brown eyes.

Jo-Jo, known as the Werewolf Boy in Adam Cole's circus sideshow, longed to be back in Guadalajara, Mexico, where they understood his language. Even though he'd been an outcast, shunned like a leper, Mexico was still his home.

The boy was born into a rural clan of Mexicans. Some of them had been struck by fate with an inherited gene where the men were born with hair all over their faces. The boy was afflicted with this excessive hairiness. The hair on his body gave him the appearance of a dog who walked upright.

By the time he was ten years old, children from other families threw rocks at him whenever he left his small hut during daylight hours. So he began to go out only at night, walking with his mother, looking for the angel star of happiness she said was waiting for him in heaven. "Everyone's got an angel star," she'd say, clutching his hand, wanting him never to lose hope.

But something had been going on between his parents that he couldn't understand. Violent, yelling arguments. Something bad was happening between them. His father would point at Jo-Jo, saying something about it being "time," then storm out of the house, leaving his mother in tears as she stroked the hair on Jo-Jo's face.

One day his father brought the priest to the house and told Jo-Jo that it was time for him to leave. That he had to go where the others of his clan who had been cursed with the same terrible problem had gone: to a sideshow. It was the only place that would have him. The only place where he could earn a living.

His mother begged and pleaded with his father, but it did no good. Jo-Jo was sold for ten dollars to a Mexican circus show operator who traveled the U.S. border towns and specialized in so-called "freaks"— humans with odd and baffling physical characteristics. Jo-Jo was locked in the back of a rickety wagon, clutching his cross. He was sold like a pig or a cow. Like a slave. The priest prayed for his soul while his father counted and recounted the money.

Jo-Jo's mother's last words were, "Everyone has an angel star, my son. Wish hard at night so your angel can find you." Tears matted the hair on his face as the wagon drove away, and he watched his mother until she was just a dot in the distance.

That was six, long years ago. He had heard later that his parents had died in a flood, leaving him alone in the world. Jo-Jo was now owned by Adam Cole, a sideshow operator with an American circus who had bought him for thirty dollars when the Mexican show had gone bust. Jo-Jo had learned English to survive. Now he was sixteen years old, without a friend in the world and no family to go back to.

One owner was no different from the other to Jo-Jo, whose job was to sit shackled in his cage in town after town, letting people spit on him and laugh at him. In exchange he was given a place to sleep, food to eat, and some money to spend in the few stores that would let him in. Though he had never stopped sending wishes up to the stars, he had come to believe that no angel was waiting for him. That if there were angels, they wouldn't listen to or look at someone with such a hairy body. He longed to go back to Mexico; in spite of the fact that his family was gone, it was still home to him. But the wagon seemed always to be taking him further and further away.

As Adam Cole's wagons rolled through the back roads of Mansfield, trying to build up the sideshow crowds, Jo-Jo looked out and saw just another small American town. He'd seen hundreds of them over the years. Nothing in America looked like Guadalajara and nothing ever would. He was resigned to never going home again; he would instead spend his life as "Werewolf Boy," a freak of nature to be exploited until the day he died.

When they had reached the outskirts of town, the wagons turned around and paraded down Main Street. Adam Cole led the way in his automobile, honking at the gawkers to keep their distance. "Get your money ready. Come see the strangest freaks in the world," he called out. He caught Jo-Jo's eyes through the bars of his cage and turned his head away. Those eyes always bothered Cole with their intensity.

Riding next to Jo-Jo's wagon, he honked, pointing to the hairy-faced boy. "This is the only werewolf in captivity. He's dangerous. He's a killer. Come to the sideshow and see for yourselves."

A stone bounced off the wagon. Jo-Jo knew it was just some kid trying to get him to peek out.

"Hey, werewolf, you in there?" a boy's voice shouted.

Jo-Jo didn't say anything. There was nothing to say. It was just another blink of a town. Another place where he would be laughed at. Another day working as a freak for Adam Cole's sideshow.

2

Drivin' Miss Beedlebottom's Car

❖

Seeing the sideshow wagons had excited Terry Youngun. Just thinking about the circus freaks, clowns, and candy was enough to drive him crazy. Or at least that was one of the excuses he'd already worked out for going joyriding in Miss Beedlebottom's car.

"I'm gonna have me a front row seat!" he shouted, honking the horn, waving to imaginary crowds. "Might even have me a wrestle with the three-legged man."

For an eight-year-old kid, Terry Youngun was a pretty good driver, even though he could hardly see over the dash.

"I'm travelin' as fast as a cat up a tree!"

Terry wasn't much for book learning, but he was commonsense smart in a devilish way. He'd dreamed up a way to drive around without going anyplace. All he had to do was take the old tire rim he'd found, put it around the barn pole in the center of the yard, knot up a length of thick rope, and secure one end to the rim and one end to the frame of the car. Then he could drive for miles without going anyplace.

Crab Apple the mule hee-hawed from the barn as the car clinkety-clanked around and around in a smoky circle. Terry honked back and shouted smugly, "You think I'll get caught, don't ya? Pa will never know!"

Miss Beedlebottom had left her brand-spanking-new car at the Younguns' house. She had some visiting to do in Springfield and had taken the train, not wanting to get her car scratched up. She was one of the biggest contributors to Terry's father's church, so watching her car was more a duty than a favor on the part of Rev. Youngun.

"Don't play around Miss Beedlebottom's car," Terry's father had warned. "Don't even touch it. Just finish your punishment chores and try to be good while we're gone."

Terry had watched as his father, his eleven-year-old brother, Larry, and six-year-old sister, Sherry, walked off toward the Springers' to eat some fresh-baked cookies. Dangit the dog had run ahead of them, howling happily. Terry was fuming because he had been left behind, so the minute they were out of sight he walked to the shiny car and came up with the idea of tying it to the barn pole.

He honked the horn six times in a row. "Just wanna have fun!" he shouted, pushing the gas pedal down until the car was flying in a circle fast enough to make a hummingbird dizzy.

Then he saw Dangit the dog come chasing over the hill, and he knew that his father must be close behind. "Gotta cover my tracks," he whispered, going over a checklist of things in his mind as he stopped the car, untied the rope, and hid it, along with the tire rim, under the hay in the back of the barn.

"Keys under the seat, car parked next to the pole. Yup, I covered my tracks good."

Then he choked. *Tracks!* There were circles of tire tracks around the barnyard. He looked up and saw Larry waving to him from the middle of the field. Behind him came Sherry on Pa's shoulders.

"Holy gosh gee-whilikers!" Terry shouted, grabbing the straw barn broom. In a swirl and twirl of dust he managed to erase the evidence. Edgar Allan Crow sat on the peak of the barn's roof squawking loudly, having a grand old time, wondering why the boy was sending mini dust devils spinning off every which way.

Terry looked around, satisfied. "Pa will never know," he nodded, proud of the stunt he had pulled.

Beezer the talking parrot came flying out of the house like a lime green Fourth of July rocket gone astray. "Redhead's in trouble!" the bird squawked.

"Shut up, bird, 'fore I have you stuffed!" Terry fumed, still mad at Sherry for teaching the fool bird to say that.

Terry looked around. *Tracks are erased. Car keys back under the seat. Barn animals fed. They'll never know.*

Then he realized that he had parked the car on the wrong side of the barn pole. *Should I move the car? Will Pa see me?* It was a do or die decision.

If he got caught this time, he would get more punishment than just a lecture. Driving the car was worse than playing on it. His pa might make good on his threat of putting Terry to work picking carrots all summer with Mr. Willard "Wormy" Reece, the farmer down the road.

Terry looked at the car. He knew it was dangerous, but he couldn't stop himself. The car had to be moved. "Not gonna work in no carrot field."

Terry raced across the barnyard and started up the car. Bashful the fainting goat keeled over as the engine sparked to life, echoing across the hill.

Rev. Youngun heard the sound and broke into a run.

The car jumped forward like a crazy root hog doing fits and stops. Terry cranked it again, got the engine going, and inched the car toward the spot where Miss Beedlebottom had left it. With just five feet left to go, the car conked out. It was in a worse place than before.

"Redhead's in trouble!" Beezer the parrot squawked as he flew from his perch on the porch.

Terry got out and tried to push the car, but he wasn't strong enough. It would take his entire school class, all six kids, to move it back to where it was supposed to be. In what he figured were the last minutes of his life, Terry cranked the car back up and stepped on the gas.

The car roared to life and the gas pedal stuck to the floor. "Oh nooooooooo!" Terry wailed.

The car flew forward, past the place where Miss Beedlebottom had left it in his pa's care. Past the barnyard. Past the point of no return.

Gotta turn this car around, Terry thought, silently sending up prayers. *Don't want no more punishment time.* Visions of spending the summer stooped over, picking carrots and knocking dirt clods off the one food he really hated, came to his mind, making him sick.

Rev. Youngun came running into the barnyard. "Oh, Lord," he whispered when he saw Terry behind the wheel of Miss Beedlebottom's runaway car. "Turn that car around!" he shouted.

"Yes, Pa." Terry spun the wheel around, bumped over a rut, lost control, and nearly fell out of the car as it went flying over the bumpy rise toward the creek.

Larry raced down the hill after the car. "Terry, stop! Turn the wheel!"

Sherry closed her eyes, screaming that Terry was going to crash. Rev. Youngun watched in horror. Things were not looking good for another big church donation this year from Miss Beedlebottom. The forty-four-year-old minister knew that if Terry crashed the car, he'd have to start looking for another line of work. Maybe even change his last name.

Terry turned the wheel back and forth, but the ruts were so deep that the car just bounced ahead like a train heading down dead-end tracks toward disaster.

"Take your foot off the gas!" Larry shouted.

"I ain't got my foot on the gas! It's stuck!"

Terry reached down, trying to unstick the pedal, but he pulled so hard that it broke loose. "Uh-oh," he moaned, watching the creek come closer and closer.

The car hit a deep hole and Terry bounced halfway out of the car. He reached over to keep from falling out and grabbed on to the wheel. The car lurched left, skimming across the edge of the creek and heading up fast toward the barn.

"Don't hurt Moo-Moo!" Sherry screamed, worried about her cow.

"Watch out, Sherry!" her father shouted. The car was heading directly toward her. Sherry shinnied up the barn pole like a pink opossum with a pack of dogs after her. Rev. Youngun ran toward the car shouting for Terry to stop, but he ended up running in circles with the car right behind him.

"Help me, Pa!" Terry screamed as he headed toward the barn.

Rev. Youngun closed his eyes. Sherry closed her eyes. Larry closed his eyes, and Dangit put his paws over his eyes. It looked for-sure certain that Terry was going to crash Miss Beedlebottom's new Oldsmobile into the side of the barn.

Terry's eyebrows touched his hairline. The barn wall disaster was just a few feet away. Crab Apple kicked out the stall rail and headed toward the field for safety. Terry knew that crashing the car was worse than driving the car, so he set his mind and prayers on coming out of this one. Holding the wheel tightly, he guided the car through the barn door with just inches to spare on either side.

Bessie the pig squealed. Bashful the fainting goat fainted dead away again. TR the turkey flew up to the loft, and Moo-Moo the pregnant cow backed up to the end of the rope that held her.

"Watch out!" Terry shouted. He steered past the milk cans and plowed through the barn right into the hay pile. The car stopped, but Terry kept going, head over heels into the hayloft, landing on top of Ratz the cross-eyed barn cat who got so scared he coughed up a hair ball on Terry's lap.

"Get off me, you dumb cat," he groaned, pushing the mush off his pants.

Rev. Youngun closed his eyes, trying to control himself, but it was no use. "Terry, you're driving me crazy! I'm at my wit's end!" he exclaimed, standing over what looked like a redheaded scarecrow all covered with dust and straw. "You understand me? You're going to be the death of me."

Terry knew from his father's all-fired-up tone that he'd better not risk making him any angrier. "Sorry, Pa."

"Do you realize that you would have ruined us financially if you'd run Miss Beedlebottom's car into the lake?" Rev. Youngun asked, the veins standing out on his neck.

"Kinda sorta."

"'Kinda sorta'? Don't you ever think about others?"

"Sorry, Pa."

"What am I going to do with you?"

"I don't know what happened, Pa," Terry whispered.

"I do. You started Miss Beedlebottom's car up."

"No, really, Pa," Terry moaned, "can't 'member a thing." He sat there rubbing his head, trying to remember how to say the word.

"What's wrong?"

"Think I've got 'nesia."

"What?"

"'Nesia, Pa. You know, the forgettin' dis-ease."

"He means amnesia," Larry said.

"You may have amnesia, but I don't. I told you to stay away from that car. Lord help me but I don't know what I'm going to do with you. I can't afford to send you to boarding school."

Sherry knew what to do. "Sell him, Pa. He almost kilt Moo-Moo."

"We can't sell Terry," Larry interjected.

"Yeah, no one would buy him," Sherry teased, sticking her tongue out.

Terry shot her an I'll-get-you-back look.

"Do you have anything to say for yourself, young man?" Rev. Youngun demanded.

The chips were down. Terry's back was against the wall. But while anyone else would have "fessed up," Terry wasn't like anyone else. Faced with the choice of telling the truth and getting punished, or fibbing and maybe avoiding punishment, there was no question about what Terry would do.

Taking a deep breath, he began his story. "Pa, I was in the barn, feedin' the animals like you told me, thinkin' 'bout the time you won me my lucky nickel, when I thought I heard someone sneakin' around the car." He paused, watching his father to see if there was any hope for his skirting of the truth.

"Go on."

Terry took that as an invitation to go for the gold. "So I snuck out, wantin' to make sure that no one touched Miss Beedlebottom's car."

"There weren't no one there," Sherry said. "You're fibbin'."

"No, as Crab Apple is my witness."

Sherry wouldn't let up. "Crab Apple can't speak."

"It's true, Pa. I thought I heard someone—a car robber or somethin'—so I snuck out and looked around. At first I didn't see nothin', but I kept hearin' a funny sound, so I looked under the car but didn't see the burglar. That's when it happened."

It was a classic Terry Youngun setup. *Feed 'em a story and hook 'em with a killer line.*

His father bit. "What happened?"

Terry grinned inside, knowing if he could skate over this thin ice he was practically home free.

"I heard a strange sound from behind the house. I figured it was a car burglar comin' to steal Miss Beedlebottom's precious car, so I looked 'round for a gun or somethin' to defend her car to my death with but I couldn't find one."

"That's 'cause the rifle's locked over at the Springers'," Larry said.

"And you knew that," Sherry added.

"Go on," Rev. Youngun sighed.

"Well, sir, not findin' a gun or sword or even a cannon or a spear or nothin' to defend the car with, I decided I should come get you to help."

"That was the right thing to do," his father nodded.

"So I got in the car and started the engine and . . ."

His father interrupted. "And that was the wrong thing to do. You should have run to the phone or raced over to the Springers'."

"But I was worried 'bout her car, seein's how we're dependin' on her church donations. Maybe I wasn't thinkin' right, but that's why I started it up—to drive the car away to protect it."

"But you don't know how to drive, son."

"I know. I didn't figure that out until I pushed on the gas and the pedal stuck."

Rev. Youngun looked off, wishing that his wife, Norma, was still alive. *She'd know what to do with this boy.*

Terry looked at his father's face and decided that he needed to pull a "Sherry." So he welled up his eyes, forcing out tears. "I was so scared, Pa," he sobbed, grabbing on to his father's leg. "I was so worried that I was gonna die that I said every prayer Ma ever taught me."

Sherry shook her head violently back and forth. "He's lyin' like a doormat, Pa."

A need to do something came over Rev. Youngun. *Guess I better go talk to Farmer Reece,* he thought, desperate to try anything to get Terry to change his ways.

"I'll be better, Pa. You'll see." Then Terry caught his father off guard. "You want to toss a baseball with me?"

"Toss a baseball? After what you just did?"

Terry looked down at his feet and whispered, "Just thought you might want to, Pa." Terry would have given away his next bag of candy if his father had just reached down and hugged him at that moment.

"I'm going to talk with Farmer Reece about you working for him. Starting tomorrow."

Tomorrow! I'll miss the circus! Terry thought. "No, Pa, I'll be good, honest," he pleaded. But it was too late. He had no idea that he had finally crossed his father's line in the sand.

3

Chained

❖

Adam Cole strutted around a promotional platform in the center of town. His balding head was slick with sweat, but he worked the crowd without letting up. At the back of the stage was a coffin, which everyone focused on.

"Ladies and gentlemen, this is just a little tease. A little taste of Cole's sideshow of forbidden delights." The large banner over the stage rustled in the breeze. It read:

ADAM COLE'S GALLERY OF FREAKS

HUMAN ODDITIES ASSEMBLED FROM
ALL OVER THE WORLD!
YOU'VE NEVER SEEN ANYTHING LIKE:
THE HUMAN TORSOS—ALICE THE HALF LADY AND
JOHNNY THE HALF BOY
KI-KOO THE BIRD WOMAN WHO SQUAWKS
JO-JO THE WEREWOLF BOY WHO GROWLS
FRANK THE THREE-LEGGED WONDER WHO CAN RUN!
PAUL THE SMALLEST MAN IN THE WORLD

"What's in the coffin?" a farm boy asked.

"I'll tell you in a moment." Cole smiled. "Now, how many of you have ever seen a three-legged man?" The crowd moved closer, shaking their heads no. "No one has, but when you come to my show, you're going to see a three-legged man, a nineteen-inch midget, a woman who looks like a bird, and Johnny and Alice, the human torsos."

"You tellin' the truth?" a farmer called out.

"Strike me down if I'm lyin'," Cole nodded.

"Prove it," the man shouted back.

"Roger, bring the picture up here." Cole waved to the side of the stage. A tall, muscular black man with a tattooed face carried out a rolled-up banner. Working together, they hung it up behind the coffin and slowly unfurled it. It was a life-size rendering titled, "Cole's Gallery of Freaks." Even the men gasped when they saw it.

"That's right! Unbelievable, ain't they?" Tapping his finger on Jo-Jo's name, Cole grinned. "How 'bout I give you just a little taste?" The crowd nodded and murmured their approval.

"You know what's in here?" he asked, standing with his foot on the coffin. "I've got the only known werewolf in captivity. The only one in the world."

"Bring him out," a drifter challenged him.

"I will, I will, but first, you've got to move back a bit 'cause this one's dangerous. No tellin' what would happen if this werewolf got loose."

The people started pushing tighter together. Goose bumps raced across their arms. Cole signaled for Roger to open the coffin. Slowly, adding drama and suspense, Roger pried open the lid with his fingers.

Cole's voice fell to a hush. "Roger, make sure that he's got his neck chain on."

"I hope it's on," Roger said, pretending to be afraid.

"Come on, what you really got in there?" a boy called out.

"A werewolf. Really. An honest-to-God werewolf," Cole asserted.

Jo-Jo pushed the coffin lid open and sprang out, doing his act. Men fell backward, women screamed, and children ran for cover as Roger struggled with the snarling, hairy young man, trying to grab the chain attached to the thick collar around Jo-Jo's neck.

"Grab him, Roger!" Cole shouted. "Don't let him get away!"

It appeared to take both men to control the boy. When they finally had Jo-Jo pushed back inside the coffin, Cole knew he was going to have a sellout crowd.

"Good job, Jo-Jo," Cole whispered into the coffin as they carried it off the stage.

Jo-Jo didn't answer, preferring the darkness to the frightened eyes of the crowd. Lying in the coffin, he smiled. In all the other towns, Jo-Jo usually let his mind go blank during his act, but now he thought of the Gomez family. They were new roadies who had signed on to work for the circus cooking tent. They were real—better than waiting for an angel to hear his prayers. It was all Jo-Jo could think about. Though he'd only known the Gomez family a few weeks, they brought back hazy, sun-warmed memories of Mexico.

In his mind, Jo-Jo relived the moment he first heard them speaking Spanish. He had stood to the side, listening, trying to remember the words they were speaking. They didn't know that Jo-Jo was from Mexico, so the family had paid him no attention, thinking he couldn't understand what they were saying.

He stood to the side, his nose remembering the sweet smells of salsa, ground cumin, chopped onions, jalapeños and rare *cabrito*—goat—simmering over the fire. Jo-Jo hadn't smelled Mexican cooking for so long that it brought back a flood of memories.

Like a rusted machine coming back to life, Jo-Jo whispered a question in Spanish: "Have you ever been to Guadalajara?"

The entire family—father, mother, and three daughters—stopped and stared at the hooded young man. Even covered by the hood, Jo-Jo's intense eyes stood out.

"Yes," said Mr. Gomez, a big burly man in stained overalls. "We have family there."

"So did I," Jo-Jo said softly.

"Come, sit down, and share our meal," Mr. Gomez offered.

Jo-Jo hesitated, long used to eating alone, but when the oldest daughter handed him a plate, he couldn't resist the smells of the crushed garlic and vinegary chopped tomatoes.

After the meal, Jo-Jo poured his heart out, sobbing when he told them about being sold. He explained that his parents, his beloved mother, had died in a flood after he had been sold.

Mr. Gomez had been in Guadalajara in those terrible days and filled in the details of how many lives had been lost in the tragedy. Jo-Jo even told them about the angel star his mother had urged him to wish on and was surprised when Mr. Gomez took his hand and held it, as if he didn't notice that it was covered with hair.

"Jo-Jo, there's an angel star for everyone," Mr. Gomez said. "Everyone. Maybe you haven't looked and wished hard enough, but it's there."

"But I used to wish every day."

"Some wishes take longer than others."

"How do you know?" Jo-Jo asked.

"Because," Mr. Gomez said, sweeping his arm across the carpet of stars in the night sky, "every star is an angel waiting to make someone's wish come true."

Jo-Jo looked down. "Even for someone who looks like me?"

"Angels love what's inside here." Mr. Gomez smiled as he touched his chest.

Jo-Jo desperately wanted to believe that was true. That even someone who looked the way he did could have an angel who would help him.

4

Maurice

❖

Maurice Springer clicked the wagon reins, scaring the neighbor's horses who whinnied as they cantered away through a field of yellow-flowered touch-me-nots. They lumbered past a grove of trees near the huckleberry bushes and set loose a pesky flock of field birds who cawed loudly. Maurice barely noticed the ruckus or heard the voices of the battling bullfrogs somewhere out on the pond. He was still miffed that his wife, Eulla Mae, had given away all his hot cookies to the Youngun kids.

"Wish she'd saved them cookies for me," he grumbled, wiping away a thin line of sweat that had beaded on the edge of his ebony chin. The breeze blew over the bushes he was passing. The sharp, tangy fragrance of chokeberries pinched at his nose, but it didn't stop him from thinking about fresh, hot cookies.

Sausage, his fat, mixed-breed dog, whimpered at the mention of food. "Now don't you go wettin' up the floorboards, gettin' all excited, thinkin' 'bout cookies you ain't gonna get," Maurice remonstrated.

Or cookies I ain't gonna get, he thought. Still, there was a custard pie waiting for him, which was better than a vinegar pie or mince pie. "Gonna have five pieces when I get home," he declared.

He waved to Sherry who came running toward the road. Maurice and his wife, Eulla Mae, were like parents to the Youngun children, taking care of them whenever Rev. Youngun was away and getting from them the love and excitement of the children they'd never been able to have themselves.

Maurice pulled the wagon to a stop. The reluctant mules took two steps extra until the front wheel came to rest in a pothole and the wagon rocked to a stop.

"Fool mules," he grumbled, then untangled his legs and looked at the girl.

"Terry's in trouble again," Sherry grinned, pushing back a comma of sun-brown hair from her forehead.

"So? What's new 'bout that? What's he sittin' in solitary confinement for this time?"

"He almost crashed Miss Beedlebottom's car."

"He what!" Maurice exclaimed.

Sherry told him what had happened, and Maurice couldn't help but break out into a grin. "That boy."

"And I heard Pa sayin' that he's gonna call Farmer Reece and put Terry to work. To learn him a lesson."

Maurice whistled. "We'll see crows fly backward 'fore we see ol' Red workin' in the carrot patch."

Sherry giggled. "Terry hates carrots."

"And he hates work too," Maurice chuckled.

Sherry shrugged. "Terry told Larry that he's gonna run away if Pa sends him to Wormy's . . . er . . . Mr. Reece's."

"Everyone calls him Wormy, that's okay."

"You think he'll run away?" Sherry asked.

"Are you askin' or are you hopin'?"

Sherry blushed. "Askin'."

"If you're askin' me, I'd say it's just kid talk. Terry's too lazy to even clean up his own dishes. Can't see him runnin' off to live off the land. Fool boy would be starved to death in a day or two."

"You think?"

"I know," Maurice said confidently. The mules snorted, wanting to move on. "Well, girl, I got to be goin'."

"Where you goin', Mr. Springer?"

"Honeybee, I got to ride to town to get some feed for my animals." Sausage woofed at the mention of food. His body was a coat of wrinkles that quivered with each woof.

"Hush, you ol' chubby thing. I ain't gettin' you food. You're fat enough."

"Sausage just likes to eat." Sherry grinned, patting the dog's head.

"That's all he ever does. Eat and wet the rugs." Maurice sighed.

❖ ❖ ❖

Maurice rode slowly toward town thinking about Terry. *I hope ol' Red's not thinkin' of doin' somethin' dumb.* He shook his head. *Boy can't be serious. He's too scared of the dark to even run to the privy at night, let alone run away from his home.*

He waved to a neighbor riding by and thought about Terry as he watched two squirrels doing a dance in the hickory trees. *Maybe I ought to let the boy come stay with us for a spell. Eulla Mae wouldn't care.*

His wife was always nice to Terry even though she thought that he was part imp, part leprechaun, and all trouble. She was the closest thing to a mother the three Youngun kids had had since their own mother had died of the fever a few years back. It didn't matter that Mrs. Springer was black and the kids were white, because the love they felt for Eulla Mae and Maurice Springer ran deeper than Willow Creek.

Maurice knew that Terry was a decent kid who just liked to have fun. *Rev. Youngun ought to take some time to see what a little guy he is 'fore he grows up and goes away. All his born days Terry's been this way. Can't ever wish back the past and change things once they is done. Man should know that, with all the preachin' he does.*

As he passed Farmer Reece's fields, Maurice saw the boys filling big burlap bags slung over their shoulders. It was hard, sweaty work. Though most of the farm kids counted their blessings if they got the chance to work at Reece's farm, Maurice knew that Terry would be counting the minutes until he could scheme a way out.

I better talk to Rev. Youngun 'bout his sendin' Terry to pick carrots. Better he might come work with me. Maurice made a face and closed his eyes, shaking his head back and forth. He pictured the potential havoc that Terry could cause if left alone. *On the other hand, can't imagine what I'd let him do that I wouldn't mind undoin'. No sir, maybe pickin' carrots would be good for ol' Red.*

There was a rush of people on the road outside of Mansfield. With the circus in town and the traveling merchants coming in to sell their wares, it looked like a Saturday crowd even though it was Thursday. Maurice saw gaudy displays and hawkers and heard loud singing from the saloon. The town was geared up for a good time.

Young farmhands and rowdies, bouncing up and down, holding on to the posts in front of Tippy's Saloon, cheered at everything and nothing. The circus wagons were going to ride through town to drum up business, and everyone was buzzing with excitement. The sound of the steam organ could be heard as the calliope was pushed from the circus grounds toward the town.

Whole families had brought box lunches to eat beside the road as they watched the parade. Women were stringing beans, and men were gathered around a pit fire where half a steer was being turned on a spit.

Maurice parked his wagon under a sun-warmed tree, next to a woman who was eating from a jar of pickled peaches. Sausage smelled the food all around him and began moaning.

"Hush, dog, you eat 'nother bite and you'll explode," Maurice warned.

He watched the ornately carved wagons and lumbering elephants pass by. "Can't wait to see the show," he said, letting the memories of circuses past bring back his youth. Sausage wouldn't stop his moaning, so Maurice relented and bought a sausage on a stick to share with the dog.

"Here," he said, "eat your cousin." The dog wolfed down the half sausage without even chewing it.

The parade finally began. Lions and tigers roared. A giraffe poked its head out through the roof of a specially built wagon. Red-faced men slapped the horses pulling the circus wagons on the rumps to keep them moving. A coal-stoked steam car tooted its horn as plumes of smoky steam rose into the air. Apple-cheeked boys jumped up onto the wagons hoping for a free peek.

Signs boasted of a "35-Horse Act," a "Man Who Wrestles Bears," "Miniature Horses That Jump Through Hoops of Fire," and a reenactment of "Jerusalem and the Crusades."

Maurice was caught up in the air of zaniness until something put his team of mules on guard. The animals snorted and lifted up their ears. At the end of the parade of circus wagons came a line of square, black wagons, led by a man in a shiny, almost new Oldsmobile.

The drivers were silent, unhappy-looking men. The man in the car barked out orders, cursing, screaming, humiliating them all as if he owned the world. Everyone looked as if they carried a load of worries on their shoulders. From the hook-nosed man with the patch on one eye driving the lead wagon, to the black driver with the tattooed face bringing up the rear, each stared straight ahead, as if there was nothing behind them but bad road and worse memories.

The sideshow performers stared out from their colorful wagons. Fingers of all shapes and sizes clutched the wooden frames, eyes peering out, like animals in the zoo. Only one wagon had bars over the window. A hairy-faced boy looked out, locked eyes with Maurice, then was gone. Maurice shuddered, feeling as if he were part of a nightmare. *What was that?* Then he saw the Werewolf Boy poster and knew. *That's something I'd hate to see in the woods.*

Maurice looked at the other sideshow pictures of circus freaks in exaggerated poses. On one a three-legged man danced. On another a werewolf with fangs was attacking a crowd. He thought he recognized the face he'd seen momentarily.

The words *Run, run, take my hand, because in the woods lives a crazy man* came to his mind. He blinked away the childhood rhyme to keep from getting the shivers, then read the sign on the wagon passing him by:

First Time to Mansfield's Harvest Festival
Adam Cole's Sideshow of Forbidden Delights.

Maurice rode behind the parade, curious as to what was inside. When the wagons went through a gate and circled around behind the show tent, Maurice halted the mules and waited. Then he eased his wagon through the gate and rode closer for a better look.

"Hey you, move along!"

Maurice turned and saw a tight-jawed man staring at him with an open glare of distaste in his eyes. It was the man who had been riding in the car at the end of the parade.

"I was just watchin' the parade."

"That's all the free looks you're gonna get," the man said, staring at Maurice with hair-trigger eyes. "I've got a business to run, and you're blockin' the way."

Maurice held back his anger. "You don't got to jump down my throat 'bout it."

Adam Cole whistled to the tall black man sitting in the lead wagon with hands strong enough to pound nails. "Roger, drive the freak wagons through town one more time. Drum up some more business."

"Yes sir," Roger said, pulling the reins back hard to turn around.

Cole turned back and looked at Maurice. "Time for you to beat it if you know what's good for you."

Maurice wanted to say something back but held his tongue, seeing that the man was not one to be trucked with. The air between them was charged.

"I'm leavin'," Maurice said, unclenching his fist.

As the freak wagons rolled past Maurice saw again the hairy-faced boy with matted fingers clutching the window bars, staring out from under the "Werewolf Boy" sign.

Simple Dream

❖

In his mind Jo-Jo was a thousand miles away. He was laughing, talking, and running with other Mexican boys. His mother waved from the top of the hill, calling him to her as if she were still alive. It was a simple, wishful dream he had over and over. A daydream that allowed him to escape from the crushing, sad life he was trapped in.

Sometimes in his dream he was normal, clean-faced, with no hair. Other times he was the way he was born. His mother was in every dream, pointing toward the stars, laughing, and shouting to Jo-Jo, "You have an angel star, son! You do!"

It was a dream that he kept to himself, willing himself to fly away to Mexico in his mind whenever he felt sad or needed to look beyond the mean and fearful faces of the crowds who came to tease him.

"I'm not a werewolf," he whispered. "I'm just a boy. I can't help the way I look."

When the wagons stopped in front of the church, Cole worked the crowd, pointing to the performers who stared out from their wagon windows. It was a crowd teaser that always worked.

Cole asked the three-legged man to sit on the ledge, then called for Paul, the knee-high midget, to climb up a rope that hung outside his wagon window and do some tricks.

Only Jo-Jo was called dangerous, an animal, someone—or something—that would rip your throat out if given the chance. A werewolf, captured alive for the world to see.

While Cole told the women and men of Mansfield about the werewolf locked inside the cage, Jo-Jo let his mind fly back to Mexico. No one could bother him there. Not even Adam Cole.

6

Railroad Jack

❖

Rev. Youngun had told Terry to clean up the mess he'd made in the barn. Life just didn't seem fair. Running away from home was sounding better and better.

"They're probably inside stuffin' their faces with cookies while I'm cleanin' up barn poo," he grumbled. "And they're probably drinkin' cold root beers and chewin' gum to clean their teeth. Bet Pa's even playin' checkers or somethin' with 'em."

He felt low-down, like he was seeing the world from a snake's point of view. "And he never has time to do nothin' fun with me. Has time to go to church lady socials and visit with sick neighbors, but he don't never have time to toss no baseball with me." Terry kicked a dirt clod into a cloud of dust. "Shoot, he probably don't even know how to throw a barn burner."

Beezer flew in squawking, "Redhead's in trouble, Redhead's in trouble."

"Get outta here!" Terry shouted, swinging the broom in the air, hoping to knock the bird down. Beezer squawked away, flying out through the loft window. "You shoulda never learned what my ignorant sister taught you," Terry yelled.

He kicked the barn wall. "I should throw that lucky nickel away. Pa probably don't even remember the time he won it for me." But Terry did. He'd relived that day at the circus a thousand times, remembering that special moment when his father had won the ring toss and presented Terry with the lucky nickel prize. It was the only time he and his father had ever done something together—just the two of them. And that was two years ago.

Crab Apple reached his head over the stall and nipped at the boy's rear. "Hey, stop that!" Terry exclaimed. The mule hee-hawed back. Then TR the turkey ran around in circles, gobbling up a storm, and Bessie the pig grunted in her pen, rooting for Terry to give her more food.

"Will you guys be quiet!"

"Why you talkin' to yourself?" a strange, gravelly voice asked suddenly.

Terry nearly jumped out of his skin. Standing before him was a stranger with five miles of bad road in his eyes. Terry looked at the hobo with his rumpled butternut suit covered with sparkling travel dust. His hair was rough-cut, like someone had tried to style it with a knife and fork. His face and eyes had more lines than a well-worn city road. His heels had long since run down until they matched the soles of his shoes. The man could have been anywhere from forty to seventy years old, and he smelled like a day-old campfire.

"Cat got your tongue?" the man asked, his cigarette-ruined voice a testament to hard living.

Terry didn't say a word.

"You got a brain or just two marbles rattlin' 'round in your head?"

"Who are you?" Terry finally blurted out.

"Don't get yourself in an uproar. I asked you first. Why you talkin' to yourself, boy?"

"Pa said I shouldn't talk to folks I don't know."

"Well then, my name's Jack, Railroad Jack. Now you know me so answer my question."

"You alone?" Terry asked, looking around.

"I travel by myself so I've always got the best company around. Now answer my question."

"Why's your voice sound funny?"

"Smoked cigarettes when I was a pip-squeak like you. Ruined my voice. Wasted a lot of years gettin' drunk and loud and makin' a fool outta myself."

"Why'd you do that?"

"'Cause I was a fool," Jack said as if anybody would know that.

Terry just kept asking questions. "How'd you get a name like Railroad Jack?"

"Hold on there, pip-squeak. Answer my question first. Why were you talkin' to yourself?"

"I don't know."

"I do. I know everythin'."

"Yeah, sure," Terry said, shaking his head like Jack was trying to pull his leg.

"Boy, I was readin' books when you were just a little tad."

"A what?"

"A tadpole. Everyone was that way once."

With a sparkle in his eye, the hobo stepped up onto an overturned box and started out like a show barker. "Ask me any question about what happened in this country. Pick a year, any year. If I get it right you owe me a shiny nickel. Stump me and I'll give you a greenback dollar."

Terry thought about his lucky nickel upstairs. Though he'd once made a vow never to lose it, always to remember the moment when his father won it for him, he now wondered if it really meant anything at all.

"Kid, you ready?"

Terry looked at the hobo. "What you shoutin' for?" he asked.

"Don't go gettin' all possessed. I like talkin' loud. Now go on, ask me a question."

Terry thought for a moment. "You know how to drive a car?"

"That's the question you want to ask the smartest man you'll ever meet in this life?"

Terry gave him a big smile. "I'll take my dollar if you don't have an answer."

"I don't know how, and I never intend to learn. I never want to get behind the wheel of one of those contraptions. Now ask me a real question."

"What are gnats doin' when they swarm around together?"

Jack looked at the boy. "Kid, I'll allow to the fact that you're probably just a squirrel brain, but see if you can try and ask me the right kind of question."

Terry stomped his foot in frustration. "Like what?"

"Ask me what happened during a certain year."

"Okay," Terry said, willing to do anything that kept him from working. "What happened back in 1816?"

The hobo grinned and winked. "You owe me five cents, boy."

Terry flinched, wondering how he'd get out of losing his lucky nickel. "You ain't told me the answer."

"You don't believe me? That'll cost you 'nother five cents."

"But you gotta answer the question 'fore I know, or give me a buck."

The hobo laughed. "Back in 1816 the U.S. Bank was chartered by Congress, the first steamboat rode the Great Lakes, and Indiana was admitted as a state."

Terry was dumbfounded. "How do you know that?"

"You already owe me a nickel, but I'll answer that for free. I read a lot. Everything I can get my hands on."

Terry didn't want to pay the man, so he figured he'd play for time, asking questions, hoping Railroad Jack would forget about the money. "How'd you know all that stuff?"

"You got wax in your ears? I told you, I read a lot."

"What do you read?"

"Anything I can get my hands on."

Terry looked around and handed him a burlap sack with printing on it. "You wanna read this?"

"You're just stallin' boy. Where's my nickel? You tryin' to get outta payin' me?"

"Nope, just curious 'bout you."

"I remember everything I read. Now give me my nickel."

"Don't got one."

Railroad Jack shook his head. "Guess I should have known that from the likes of you with all that red hair."

"What 'bout the likes of you?" Terry caught a whiff of the man. "Think you need a bath."

"I never take baths, and I don't wear socks," Jack said, lifting up one of his ankles proudly.

"And that's why you're travelin' alone, 'cause you smell bad."

"Smell don't bother me and since I travel alone, I'm all I got to worry about."

"You're a fancy-talkin' hobo."

"And proud to be one." Jack bowed like a dandy. "That's why my name's Railroad Jack. I travel the rails of life learnin' everythin' I can."

He turned around. Lettered on the back of his knapsack was, "Railroad Jack—World's Champion Memory Expert!"

Then he spun back and asked Terry, "So what's your name, son, and why you talkin' to yourself?"

"Give me a buck."

"Why?"

"'Cause you asked me my name."

The hobo chuckled. "Think you're a sharp cookie, don't ya'?"

"Wish I had me a cookie. There's a pile of 'em inside, but I don't get any. My brother and sister do but I don't."

"That's 'cause you've been bad again."

"How'd you know?"

"I know everythin'. You don't have to get kicked in the head by the same mule twice to learn to step around his backside."

"What's that supposed to mean?"

"It means I know you're a troubled kid."

"I ain't troubled," Terry said defensively.

"But you're in trouble, ain't ya?"

Terry couldn't look the man in the eyes. He felt like he'd just been slapped with a fifty-dollar put-down. "Mind your own beeswax."

"I also know you're a tricky kid who just got outta payin' me that nickel you don't want to part with." Railroad Jack was good at guessing and Terry wasn't hard to figure out. "That nickel you were savin' to buy candy with."

"You do know everythin'! Are you a magician?"

"Don't take magic to be smart. Just gotta read, that's all."

"What's my name?"

Railroad Jack winked. "Red. Just like your hair."

"Don't like that nickname. My name's Terry Youngun."

"Nothin' wrong with red hair. Shows you got roots." Jack hitched up his pants, kicked the dust off his shoes against the barn wall, and opened his canteen. "Well, son, if you won't pay me the nickel you owe me, will you give me a cold fill?"

Terry worked the barn pump until the silt and rust had washed out, then filled up the canteen. "You hungry?"

"Nope. I ate my noon meal of leftovers that a nice widow lady 'bout five miles back gave me. Won't need to eat again 'till my stomach growls Dixie."

"Wish I could eat when I wanted to," Terry said. "Wish I could be like you." He sighed. "Wish I could travel with you for a few days."

Jack shook his head. "I don't travel with no one."

"Where you goin'?"

"Got a lot more of America to see," Jack said, as he walked away whistling.

"How you gonna see it if you can't drive?" Terry asked, tagging along.

Jack looked down with an amused look. The boy brought back memories of himself. "I like to ride the rails. Travel for free."

"Can I go with ya?"

"No. You're just a kid and I travel alone. Told you that, didn't I?"

"Wish I was goin' along," Terry said, looking at the hobo and then back at his house.

"Don't be talkin' claptrap like that."

"Well, it's true. I'm tired of livin' 'round here."

"Don't be sayin' that," Jack cautioned.

"My head's filled up with don'ts and warnings. I want to live free like you."

Jack coughed, then cleared his throat. "Freedom puts speed into your legs if you know where you're goin', but if you're just runnin' away, you never get far 'cause you're always runnin' from yourself."

Terry wasn't sure what Jack had just said. He suspected that the hobo was a bit wacky. He looked back toward the house. "And they're eatin' cookies in the kitchen and won't give me a one."

Jack placed his hand on Terry's shoulder. "Kid, you got a fine-lookin' home and probably a finer family. Go in there and work things out."

"And a pa that don't have time to do nothin' with me."

"You're just gripin' for nothin'. There's nothin' like a home to come back to in this life. Ask me and I'll tell you that."

"Do you got a home to go home to?"

Jack stopped and looked off. "Wish I did, but I left without sayin' good-bye. Thought I knew everything there was to know."

"But you do."

"Nope, son, I don't. I might be book smart, but I sure wasn't people smart. Never leave without sayin' good-bye 'cause it might be the last time you'll ever see your folks again, and you'll never get a chance to say what you shoulda said."

"Why don't you go back and see 'em? Your folks I mean." As soon as he asked the question, Terry thought he saw the hobo's eyes tear up.

Moving quickly to escape from that dark corridor of his mind, Jack forced back the mist that had enveloped his eyes. "Can't, son. They died from cholera soon after I left."

"Why didn't you say good-bye?"

"That's a question no book can answer. But in all my travels I ain't never found a place better than the one I left." Jack slowly rubbed his eyes as if he were trying to erase the visual memory. "All I know is that I left to climb the hill of my choosing but found I came down a mountain of memories that never seem to end."

"But you might have died too if you'd stayed," Terry said, matter-of-factly.

"Maybe, maybe not. All I know is that I'll never have the chance to know what would have happened." Jack dusted off his dirty pants. "Red, remember that you're never gonna know what's down the road ahead of you, but you always got the choice to change direction. See you, kid."

Terry watched the odd man walk off down the road and wished he were going with him.

7

Cole's Plan

❖

When the promotional ride through Mansfield was over, Cole pulled the tarp over his car to keep the dust off. Standing beside the Oldsmobile, he patted the car gently. He loved it more than life itself. It was the only possession he owned debt free. And no one was to touch it. Not even his performers.

Inside his wagon, he sat under the flickering lantern, tracing his finger over the map, brooding about his life. He sucked on a piece of hard candy, his cold, steel-blue eyes humorless, so somber that he looked older than his years. Cole's jaw was tight, straining with his thoughts of worries that he couldn't shake.

Smashing his fist down, he shouted, "If it doesn't work, then someone's gonna get hurt! I won't live in debt like this anymore."

Adam Cole's Gallery of Freaks was a traveling show that went from town to town across the country on the county fair circuit. Cole's collection of deformed people, which he called "The Largest Gallery of Human Oddities Ever Assembled from the Far Corners of the Earth," were treated more like cattle than human beings.

Though the grotesque collection of what some called "oddities" and "monstrosities" disturbed the feelings of many in the communities where it stopped, Cole knew it touched and revealed secret weaknesses. It gave people a chance to step out of their everyday lives, their everyday existences, and enter the world of the monstrous, fantastic, and provocative.

Everywhere there was controversy. When churches and newspapers railed against the inhumanity of the shows, it just increased the attendance. Opening with the famous Freaks of Life dance that Cole had created, his show was a "must see" in small towns across the Midwest. Cole had assembled a troop of human oddities that brought in top dollar. And it would have made him rich if he hadn't gambled it away. Cole had spent all his adult life finding and displaying deformed and disfigured people in small towns throughout the Midwest, but he had nothing to show for it except debt and the prospect of years of work just to break even.

Adam Cole was a complex and dangerous man. Raised in a troubled family, he had left behind him a trail of hurt and maimed people as a testament to his hatred. Rubbing his balding head, which glistened under the swaying wagon lamp, and pulling at the wisps of hairy nothingness, he blew a long, fluttering breath through his lips. His pale, thinning hair stuck to the sides of his scalp in thin wisps.

"I'm tired of bein' in debt," he sighed, thinking about the money he still owed to Mr. Stein, the circus owner, who had covered his gambling debts. Cole's passion and weakness was for the snap of cards, the thump of dice, and piles of winning chips. He'd been on a winning streak until he lost it all in Springfield, Missouri, and now he was fighting to pay it back.

I'm tired of playing these hick towns. Wish I were in Mexico. They'd treat me like a king down there.

From everything he'd read and heard, the freak show owners in Mexico were much sought after by the wealthy landowners for private showings. Cole thought back on what the Mexican operator who had sold him Jo-Jo had said: "Come to Mexico and you'll be rich, Mr. Cole. They'll love your show down there."

"My freaks would be worth their weight in gold in Mexico," Cole whispered. "And Jo-Jo knows the language." *Just wish that boy's eyes weren't so intense. Weren't so . . . so scary.* He hated to look at the Werewolf Boy's face—he was the only freak that truly disturbed him. But he'd need Jo-Jo's language skills in Mexico.

Cole needed money, a lot of money, and he would do anything to get it. He wanted to escape, to get out from under the debt hanging over him and start life over, but he knew that the circus owner would track him down and confiscate his sideshow to cover the debt.

"If I can just get across that Mexican border without Stein or his thugs catchin' me, I'll have it made. They'll come from miles around to see Adam Cole's show down there."

All Cole needed was money, enough either to pay his debt to Stein or pay his way to Mexico. Looking at the map spread out under the lantern, he went over the details of the plan he was formulating in his mind. He was determined to see it through, no matter what it took or who he hurt.

Jo-Jo pulled the hood over his face and walked among the sideshow wagons. He was not allowed to leave the small area. Hiding his face was the only way he could go out during the day without drawing the attention of the local gawkers.

I want to see the Gomezes. Talk to them. Hear their laughter. They were his link to Mexico, his bridge home, but now he was worried. Mr. Gomez had told him they were going back to Mexico.

They're leaving. They're leaving me.

It was the second time in his life that Jo-Jo's heart had truly ached. He never thought he'd feel the same hurt as when his parents had sold him, but the Gomezes had treated him like he was a member of their family. Like he was a human being. He didn't want them to leave, but he didn't have the nerve to run away from Cole and go with them.

When he found no one at their camp, he panicked, thinking they had already left. Then he realized that they were off working at the cooking tent, so he snuck back to his wagon before Cole noticed he was missing.

Cole looked at the map of Mansfield again, memorizing the streets and alleys. "This plan is gonna work. I know it will."

It really didn't matter which town it happened in. Each rube town was the same. All he needed was courage—which he'd finally found. The courage to break free and settle his debt with Stein one way or another. With money or the point of a gun.

"And if he won't settle with me then he'll settle for a bullet," he mumbled, biting his lip.

He put the map away and headed out the door to canvass the town again. He passed a Mexican roadie who'd been following the circus doing pickup work. Cole didn't even remember the man's name.

"How's Jo-Jo, Mr. Cole?" Mr. Gomez asked in halting English.

Cole had seen the man talking through the barred window on Jo-Jo's wagon. "He'll do fine if you leave him alone. He don't need to be thinkin' about places he'll never see again."

"But he just wanted to talk Spanish and . . ."

"And I told you, all you're doin' is upsettin' him."

Cole pushed Gomez to the side and continued on his mission. He was looking for hoboes—he needed them for his plan. He'd seen them along the railroad tracks, hard men without illusions. Mutilated veterans too old and sotted to remember the Civil War that had left them maimed. Walking around the back of the train station, Cole stood in the shadows and watched the greasy-haired hoboes who were passing a jug around.

Cole focused on the sullen faces. *They're perfect. Perfect for what I got planned. Jail will be a step up for these losers.*

Cole saw the Mansfield sheriff leaning against a light pole on the station platform. "You better keep an eye on them shiftless tramps," he said casually. "They'll steal the pennies off a dead woman's eyes."

"They won't pull nothin' on my watch," Sheriff Peterson said flatly.

"I hope not," Cole smiled, handing the sheriff two free tickets to his freak show. He walked back toward his wagon, wondering if one gun would be enough to accomplish his plan.

8

Forbidden Leaflet

❖

Terry sat in the back of the barn behind the pile of hay, reading the sideshow handbill: "The Largest Gallery of Human Oddities Ever Assembled from the Far Corners of the Earth!" The freak pictures seemed naughty, like something he shouldn't be looking at, which was exactly why Terry had it in his hand.

Can't wait to see the freak show, he thought. The circus was in town for only one more day, which was enough time to go see the sideshow and play ring toss again with his father. *I want him to win me another lucky nickel.* Terry nodded, remembering the moment two years back when his father had handed him the lucky nickel prize.

Pa said that if my heart's in the right place, the nickel will take me to faraway places. All I want is for it to take me to the circus tomorrow.

As punishment for driving Miss Beedlebottom's car, Rev. Youngun had said that Terry would have to stay home instead of going to see the circus. But Terry didn't believe his father would actually keep him from going. The whole family was going to town tomorrow. *Pa will give in. He always does. Even if he don't wanna toss a ball, he ain't mean 'nough to keep his own kid from goin' to the circus.*

That he was sure of. As night follows day Terry knew in his heart of hearts that he'd be going to the circus. *Can't wait to eat all that taffy and cotton candy and gumdrops.*

He closed his eyes and could smell the mud and sawdust. In his mind he was eyeballing all the excitement. The food and game booths. The carnies calling out to guess your weight. Ring toss. Pony rides. Fortune-tellers.

"I can smell the buttered popcorn," Terry whispered, licking his lips. He didn't hear his brother and sister sneaking up behind him.

Larry pointed to the pile of hay and gave Sherry a nod. Sherry crept over toward Terry. "What you doin'?" she asked, kicking back the hay.

"Nothin'," Terry mumbled, looking closely at the strange pictures on the sideshow flyer. The picture of Werewolf Boy made him shiver.

"What are you lookin' at that for?" Sherry taunted. "Pa said you're not goin'."

"Says you. I says I'll be goin'."

"But Pa said . . ."

"Pa always says that," Terry said, giving her a friendly shove. "Ain't no good pa ever born would keep his son from goin' to the circus." He touched the picture of Werewolf Boy. "Even his pa would let him go."

"He's already in the circus," Larry said.

Terry stared at the picture of the hairy boy. He held the flyer up to the light. "Says here that a hippo-pot-a-mus is comin' with the circus. What's a hippo-pot-a-mus?"

"You know," Larry shrugged.

"I don't know. That's why I'm askin' you."

"I think it's a bird," Larry mumbled.

Sherry came flying over the hay pile and grabbed the flyer, but Terry snatched it back. "Pa told you not to look at that," she whined, "I'm tellin'."

"You do and I'll stick a spider in your mouth when you're asleep."

"You will not."

"Will to. I'll stick a big spider who'll make a web over your mouth and nose so you suf-cate to death."

Sherry ran off crying. Larry shook his head at his younger brother. "You're in trouble now."

"So what? I'm in so much trouble now that my behind's gonna root to the corner. Anyway," he shrugged, "I'm thinkin' 'bout runnin' away and bein' a hobo."

"You wouldn't."

"*You* wouldn't but I would. Bein' a bum sounds better than workin' like a dog 'round this place."

Larry frowned. "Pa's gonna be mad if he hears you talkin' like that."

"So, I'm mad at him." Terry started to tell his brother about Railroad

Jack but didn't. Instead, he put his finger on the picture of the man with three legs. "You think that's real?"

Larry wanted to turn away, but he couldn't help looking at the picture again. "Pictures don't lie."

"Why three legs?" Terry wondered aloud to himself. "Seems like havin' three arms would be better."

"Don't think he had much choice," Larry muttered.

Terry pointed to the picture of the man with no legs. "What 'bout that? Looks like someone just cut the picture in half."

Larry shrugged. "Guess you'll never know."

Terry guffawed quietly. "Heck yeah, I'll know! I'm goin' to see for myself."

"Pa won't let you," Larry exclaimed.

Terry ran his finger down the pictures, reading the captions. "Will you look at these things?"

Terry's eyebrows raised at the pictures of the strange people. He gazed at the picture of Jo-Jo the Werewolf Boy. "Looks like a two-legged mutt." Then he whistled. "Man alive, if I ever got locked into a room with the likes of him, I'd have me a sure-as-shootin' heart 'tack."

"That ain't nice."

Terry didn't care. "Werewolfs would rather rip your throat out than shake your hand." Tapping the picture, he looked at Larry. "Can't imagine trying to give him a shave." Then he giggled to himself. "Think he chases cats?"

Larry just shook his head. "They're 'werewolves' not 'werewolfs.'"

"That's what I said," Terry nodded.

They both heard a noise. "Put that away 'fore Pa catches you," Larry whispered.

Terry took a quick look at Paul the nineteen-inch midget standing next to the three-legged wonder. "Which one do you think could run faster?"

Larry gave him a questioning look. "What are you talkin' about?"

Terry pointed to the pictures. "Do you think the three-legged wonder man can run faster than the midget?"

"How the heck should I know?" Larry frowned.

Terry pondered having three legs. "Larry," he said very seriously, "where do you get three-legged underpants?"

Larry coughed, wide-eyed. "Three-legged underpants?"

"I've never even seen three-legged pants." Terry paused, then asked, "And who makes three-footed shoes?"

Larry turned away, ignoring him.

"Do you think his third leg is right-footed, left-footed, or straight-footed?"

"Pa's gonna punish you if you keep talkin' 'bout that sideshow," Larry admonished in a harsh whisper.

"Gosh, I'm *just* curious."

"Curiosity killed the cat," Larry said, his eyes straight ahead.

"Terry, have you finished your work?" Rev. Youngun asked loudly as he stepped into the barn.

"Just workin' on the hay pile," Terry said, stuffing the flyer into his pants. He looked at Larry, giving him a don't-rat look.

"Come out from behind there. Sherry said you were looking at something bad."

"Sherry's just a rat," Terry said, looking around frantically. He took the *Farmer's Almanac* off the nail next to the bench and walked out.

"What were you looking at?" Rev. Youngun asked.

"This," Terry said. "Just wanted to do a little reading."

Rev. Youngun scolded Sherry for exaggerating all the way back to the house.

9

Nickel Game

❖

Railroad Jack made his way through Mansfield, thinking about the squirrelly, redheaded kid. "Imagine, him wantin' to run away and travel with me." He'd traveled alone for as long as he could remember, but he had to admit that he had enjoyed talking with the boy. "Didn't know that a kid could be so crazy. Must have somethin' to do with his jim-bob red hair."

Jack read everything he could get his hands on and memorized road signs, so he always knew where he was going and where he had been. He was blessed with a memory that sponged up everything.

Jack saw that the circus was in town, which meant that there'd be a lot of nickels to pick up. Making his way through the crowd of afternoon shoppers grown twice as large because of the circus, he stopped at the town square, looking around for a place to set up his platform. He saw the library and wanted to go in and read, but he needed money if he was going to eat.

From the looks of the crowd, farmers had come in from miles around to load up on food and supplies and go to the circus. There was still a touch of the Old West in the looks of the hunters who sat outside the butcher shop, waiting to sell the deer they brought in strapped to their mules.

Bedal's General Store was holding a sale for Queensware crockery and St. Louis shoes. Jack peeked through the window at the shelves filled with coffee, chocolate, dried legumes in bushel baskets, and more canned goods than he knew existed. A woman was filling up her own jar from the spigot of the molasses barrel.

Two doors down, Chan's Chinese Store was advertising tea, canned fish, firecrackers, and exotic cures. Jack peeked into the butcher shop, which had hunters and customers lined up on both sides of the room. Besides the usual pork and beef, the butcher's assistant was busy writing up signs for bear steak, venison, and prairie chickens.

"Wish I had me a good plug of jerky and some sassafras tea," Jack said, pushing down the wooden sidewalk. His stomach was grumbling for food. A fresh, hot, sit-down meal.

"Guess I better find a place to start earnin' nickels then," he mumbled.

"I know you," an old black hobo said, pulling at Jack's arm.

"A lot of folks know me. I'm famous."

"Met you down in Memphis. You put on quite a show."

Jack squeezed his eyes shut, putting his finger to his temple deep in thought. "You talkin' about the time I answered three hundred and thirty-two questions nonstop?"

"Thought it was jest thirty-two," the old man chuckled.

"No, to my recollection it was more than that."

"My name's Skeeter. Skeeter Nelson."

"Is that the name your mama gave you, or were you hatched like a skeeter?"

"Real name's Elijah, but I used to run 'round so fast that my daddy named me Skeeter."

"You already know my name, Mr. Mosquito," Jack said.

"Skeeter's just a nickname my daddy gave me."

"Glad you told me," Jack said. The man looked lean and hungry. Jack didn't need anyone hanging around him. "Nice jawin' with you but I gotta be movin' on."

"How 'bout I travel right 'long with you? It'd be good to have a smart man to talk to."

"Nope," Jack said, waving the man away, "I travel alone."

"Is it 'cause I'm black?"

Jack shook his head. "You think color means somethin' to a hobo? We're all from the same hungry cloth."

Skeeter leaned forward, looked Jack in the eye, then stood back, seeing that the man had seen trouble in his life. "You need someone to unburden yourself to?"

"I got myself to talk to."

Skeeter shrugged. "Well, if you change your mind and need a good listenin' buddy, I'll be around."

With his burlap carry sack in hand, Skeeter walked away. He turned once to look at Jack before he was lost in the crowd of shoppers.

Jack liked to talk to crowds, but he had never had a friend he could open up with. So he traveled alone, carrying a burden too heavy for any one person. As he'd told Terry, his greatest regret was leaving home without saying good-bye, without telling his mother and father that he loved them. That guilt haunted him. When Jack thought about his mother, his eyes were alive with painful memories.

She would have understood if I'd just told her I wanted to make my own way, he thought. His mother had lectured him that there were no roads paved with gold, but Jack thought he knew better and had pretended that he was going into town when he was really leaving home.

"I intended to come back. I just wanted to make some money first," he muttered, trying to convince himself. It didn't work.

The last words he could remember his mama saying as she pushed back her pince-nez glasses were, "When you comin' home, Jack?"

When you comin' home, Jack? he thought, his eyes misting up.

Though he'd been over it thousands of times in his mind as the clackety-clack train rails crisscrossed the country under him, Jack had never come to peace with himself for leaving without saying good-bye. That was why he traveled alone, moving from town to town, trying to stay one step ahead of the memory that was always shadowing him.

Jack looked around for an old box to stand on, but there were none in any of the alleys. The sky had an odd, greenish hue, hinting of rain to come, but Jack figured he could make a few nickels before the first drops fell. Enough to buy a couple of beef dodgers.

Behind the saloon where the ticky-tacky piano was playing, he found a good box and dragged it into the street. As if he were setting up shop, he drew a square in the dust with his boot around the box, adjusted the angle so that it was parallel with the sidewalk, then started calling out for business.

"Ladies and gentlemen, gather 'round. My name is Railroad Jack, the man you've read about. The man the St. Louis papers call the tramp genius."

"What you sellin'?" shouted a man with a wild head of hair that looked like a fuzz ball.

"I'm not sellin' anything, pincushion head. I'm trying to give money away."

"Well, we're waitin' to clean your clock," a merchant with a paunch and a turkey neck shouted.

"That's what I want," Jack nodded. "I just want to give money away."

"Probably givin' away Confederate money," a bifocaled beanpole of a man guffawed, spraying spittle on the old woman in front of him. The crowd chuckled.

"No, real money. U.S. greenbacks," Jack said, holding up the one and only dollar bill he had left.

That got everyone's attention. As Jack continued his patter the crowd began growing. Voices, murmurs, and gibberish crossed and crisscrossed through the growing street corner assembly.

"Listen up. I'm gonna prove that I know more than any of you about this country." A few in the crowd chuckled, figuring it was just a come-on as Jack went into his pitch.

Tippy, the owner of the saloon, came out and listened to Jack's patter, smiling like a contented cat. He rapped his sharp knuckles against the building's wooden door frame to get Jack's attention.

"I'll go the nickel with you. Matter of fact, I'll go twenty nickels with you."

Jack turned around and sized the man up. Tippy was dashingly dressed like a dandy, and Jack figured he didn't care much either way if he won the dollar or not but was along just for the fun of it.

"What's your question?" Jack asked.

"What year was Nevada admitted to the Union?"

"That's easy, 1864."

The crowd looked to Tippy to see if Jack was right. Tippy nodded and handed him a nickel. "You're pretty smart."

"That's nothin'," Jack grinned, swelling up with pride. "You want to know what else happened that year?"

Tippy chuckled at the man's audacity. "Sure."

"Well sir, Sherman marched to the sea, burnin' down Atlanta, and the battles at Wilderness, Spotsylvania, Cold Harbor, and Petersburg cost Grant sixty-eight thousand wounded and dead soldiers."

Most of the folks in the crowd looked around at each other in amazement. Tippy asked another question, happy to hand over his nickels to build up the crowd. Then he stepped back as the questions flew from the crowd and Jack's pocket filled up with nickels.

By the time he was finished, Jack had thirty nickels in his pocket, and Tippy had twenty new customers in his saloon. When the crowd of backslappers began to thin out, Jack said he needed to take a water break. Tippy walked up and slapped him on the back. "That nickel game you're running is darn good. You with the circus or somethin'?"

"Nope. Just do what I do to get my nickels so I can keep on travelin'."

"You want a job workin' for me?"

"Doin' what?"

"Entertainin'. I'll pay you a hundred dollars a week to show up each night and answer questions in the saloon. And I'll let you keep all the nickels you earn and back you when you lose."

Jack hesitated, then shook his head. "Nope. I turned down a vaudeville agent who offered me a thousand dollars to go on tour. So if I turned down a thousand your hundred don't even make me blink twice."

Tippy couldn't help but admire the eccentric man. "You're some piece of work. Well, if you change your mind, the offer still stands."

Jack stepped toward the edge of the sidewalk, not noticing that Skeeter Nelson was following him, bound and determined to be Jack's traveling companion. Jack didn't look where he was going and stepped off the sidewalk into the path of a car.

Skeeter pulled him back as the honking car sped past. "You ought to be careful. You need me to be walkin' along beside you to keep you from gettin' runned over."

Jack blew a stream of fluttering air in frustration. "Can't get used to them things. They're dangerous." He turned, focused, and saw it was the old man again. "What do you want?"

"Just thought you'd changed your mind."

"About what?"

"About lettin' me be your travelin' companion. Smart man like you shouldn't be travelin' alone. You need someone to listen to you."

Jack smiled at the compliment. With a pocketful of nickels, he felt like sharing the wealth with a fellow hobo. "When's the last time you ate good?"

"Don't have a memory like you do to remember that far back."

"Then let's go over to that café and have us a plate lunch. On me."

"Sure they'll let us hoboes in?" Skeeter asked, sniffing at Jack.

"As long as we show 'em our money first."

"When's the last time you took a bath?"

"I don't take baths. They're bad for your health."

"But they sure make you smell better, if you know what I mean," Skeeter said, crinkling his nose.

"If it don't bother me don't let it bother you. Besides, I'm the one who's payin' for the grub."

Over cups of hot coffee and heaping plates of crackling corn bread, sliced barbecue pork, and mashed potatoes, Jack and Skeeter told their brags, what-ifs, and whatevers. They were noisy, animated eaters. Both of them had crossed paths with some of the more colorful hoboes riding the rails, and now they had crossed paths with each other.

Jack watched Skeeter wolf down two platefuls. "You part tapeworm?"

"Nope, just kinda hungry I guess." Skeeter looked at what some of the other customers were eating. "Sure wish I had me a plate of baked beans, some bean soup, and maybe some bean porridge."

"And you'd blow this town off the map," Jack said.

"Yes sir," Skeeter said, seeing some inner memory. "I remember bein' a little boy, skippin' 'round as my mama and I sang:

"Bean porridge hot,
Bean porridge cold,
Bean porridge in the pot,
Nine days old."

Jack smiled. "You start skippin' 'round, singin' that in here and they'll put you in the nuthouse."

For the first time in his life Jack knew he was tired of traveling alone. He wanted someone to talk to. After the meal, they walked through Mansfield. Skeeter listened as Jack began talking about the memory that had bothered him for so many years.

Money

❖

Taking a piece of sucking candy from the bag in his drawer, Cole counted his money for the third time. *Maybe if I puff up my show I can get Flossy or some of those Barnum boys to buy me out. Pay off all my debts and just start again.*

His only mistake had been hitching up with Stein's circus three years ago and borrowing the money to pay off his gambling debts. Now Stein owned the title to his sideshow and was threatening to take it over if Cole missed a payment.

Smashing his fist down on the table in frustration, Cole wished he could have it all. He wanted his show, his debts paid, and the freedom to start again in Mexico. He wanted to ride through the poor sections of the country, waving like an emperor from his car. *Everyone down there would know me as the king of the sideshow business.* But he knew there was no easy way out. "It's Stein or me," he whispered, going over his plan, thinking about the gun in his desk drawer.

"I know it'll work," he mumbled to himself.

"You say somethin', boss?" Roger asked as he opened the back door.

"Just talkin' to myself," Cole answered, wondering how far he could trust his main wagon driver.

Roger was big and mean and had done prison time for beating a man half to death during an argument. He was the kind of man, like Cole, who would do anything for money.

"Roger, you keep an eye on things. I gotta go work the town and drum up some more business," Cole ordered.

❖ ❖ ❖

Maurice finished up his errands and tied a load of feed down on the back of the wagon. He took the long way through town, avoiding the crowd in front of Tippy's Saloon. Cutting through the back alleys, he was surprised at all the transients who had come to town, following the circus like flies. At the corner of Main Street and Commerce, he pulled to a halt in front of the bank and tied the team up.

"Hey, Maurice," Sheriff Peterson called out, "you in town for the circus?"

"Nope, I'm comin' back tomorrow. Bringin' the Youngun kids with me."

"Bring plenty of money then." The sheriff chuckled good-naturedly. "Those kids know how to eat candy."

"You don't need to be tellin' me that. That's why I hardly got any egg money left in my secret sock."

Neither man paid any attention to Cole's car approaching.

"And you best hold tight to your money," the sheriff said. "There's a bunch of hoboes hangin' 'round the train station, half corned on sour mash."

"I saw a pack of 'em in the alleys."

"They're everywhere," the sheriff said. "Bet there'll be a lot of things missin' from folks' yards after they leave town."

"I hope not."

"Keep your eyes open for me. I'm worried 'bout all these no-good hoboes."

"I will," Maurice nodded, turning toward the bank. He took a couple of steps but was bumped aside at the doorway by a gruff man whose voice was barbed-wire tight.

"Watch where you're goin'."

Maurice saw it was the rude man from the sideshow. "You watch where *you're* goin'," he retorted.

Adam Cole glared at Maurice for a moment, as if thirty wildcats were waiting to spring out from behind his eyes. He fought for control, then changed, allowing his deep charisma to mask his true feelings. Maurice felt a curious tingle as he looked into the man's eyes.

"Sorry, sir," Cole said, dusting Maurice off.

"That's all right," Maurice shrugged, taken aback by the man's change in tone.

"Here, let me give you a couple of tickets to the sideshow. How many you need?" Cole said, showing a smile of teeth.

Maurice was flustered, ashamed of himself for judging the man.

"You are goin' to my show, aren't you?" Cole asked.

"Your show?"

"I'm Adam Cole," he said, handing Maurice a flyer. "I own the show." He flashed another smile. His secret, wicked charm was an act that came naturally.

Maurice looked at the circular. "Is Piramai Sami still performing?"

Cole shook his head. "Wish he was. Made a small fortune off him when he toured with me."

"Where'd he go?"

"Back to India. I hear he's a raji or king or somethin' like that back there. Got hisself a harem of wives."

"That was the strangest-lookin' man I ever saw," Maurice said.

"Then you need to see my new act. I want to make up to you for my rude behavior."

"You don't got to do nothin'," Maurice said.

"I've got freaks you wouldn't believe. Now how many tickets you need?"

"For free?"

"For free," Cole grinned.

"Would five be too many?"

"Five it is," Cole said, putting them into Maurice's shirt pocket. "And keep your pocket buttoned. Looks like a lot of seedy thieves have come to town," he said, nodding toward the down-and-out-looking group of men standing between the buildings across the street. "It's a sin to Moses the way they try to come 'round decent folks."

"They work for the circus?"

"Nope. Some of them help put the tent up and down. But most of them are here for no good." Cole held the bank door open for Maurice. "Now, after you."

Maurice thought it was his lucky day and watched how Cole charmed the two tellers, passing out tickets for the next day's show.

"It's the last show of the year, ladies," Cole said. "Be sure to come."

He even gave Mr. Givens, the bank manager, a handful of tickets to give to any employees who might be off for the day.

"You don't have to do this, Mr. Cole," Mr. Givens said.

"It's good promotion. That's the way ol' P. T. Barnum himself built his name. Everyone's gonna be there for the last show. Even the sheriff himself."

"The circus seems to have done quite well this year. The town merchants have been making some big deposits," Mr. Givens said.

"That's 'cause they want you to protect their money."

Givens shrugged. "In Mansfield, it hardly needs protecting. We haven't had a bank robbery since the bank opened in 1880, and to my memory, there's never been a store robbed in these parts."

"Never can be too careful, Mr. Givens. I bet I've traveled through a thousand Mansfields in my time, and the folks in every one of 'em think they live in a magic town where nothin' bad ever happens."

"Thanks for your concern, but it's a safe bet this town will stay peaceful."

"Way things are goin' in this life, I wouldn't bet nothin' but Confederate money on that." Cole pointed to the dull-eyed hoboes hanging around the alley outside. "Them hoboes are crafty thieves. I'd ask the sheriff to keep an eye on them bums if I was you."

Givens looked outside, then back at Cole. For a quick moment a mild alarm went off in his mind. Was there something dangerous hidden below the surface of the circus man? But Cole's quick smile dispelled the fear.

Railroad Jack walked past the bank window not knowing that Adam Cole was memorizing his face. Behind him walked Skeeter, still humming his bean song. "That's a thief if I ever saw one," Cole said disgustedly. "You remember that man's face. He looks like trouble to me."

Givens looked but didn't pay Jack much attention. He figured that Cole was just agitated about the hoboes.

Cole saw that Maurice was about to leave and asked him, "You want a ride back to the circus in my car?"

"No sir, my wagon's just out there."

"Remember what I said. Keep your pocket buttoned and your wallet out of sight. There's a lot of varmints around."

"I'll remember that," Maurice said, thinking about the free tickets in his pocket.

Cole watched Maurice exit, wondering if there was some way he could hook him into his plan. He turned and gave Givens one of his hundred-dollar smiles. "Like I said, you all come to the show tomorrow. I guar-and-darn-tee-ya it'll be one you'll never forget."

Givens watched him leave the bank and drive away, wondering why he had such an uneasy feeling about the man. Cole eyeballed Jack and Skeeter as he drove past them. Skeeter tipped his imaginary hat and kept right on singing:

"Bean porridge hot,
Bean porridge cold . . ."

Jack elbowed him. "If you wanna travel with me, you gotta learn some other song."

Cookie Thief

❖

After finishing his chores, Terry sat by himself upstairs, flipping his lucky nickel in the air. He listened to his father talk and laugh with Larry and Sherry. They were having a grand old time eating Mrs. Springer's cookies in the kitchen. In his mind they were all face down on the cookie plate, licking and hogging up all the sweets that should have been his.

"Bet they've got some secret box of cakes they've been holdin' out on me," Terry fumed. "Bet Mrs. Springer made them some cakes and pulled candy . . . probably a couple of custard pies too."

He heard Sherry shout, "Let's make ice cream!" and Terry thought he was going to have a heart attack.

"Ice cream," he whispered, closing his eyes and wanting to cry. He waited to see if Larry was sent to the icehouse to get an ice block out of the sawdust to begin the process.

"Do we have enough coarse salt?" his father asked.

Terry put his hands over his ears. "I'm gonna faint," he whispered as he imagined them all shoveling the ice cream down with their spoons. His throat was tight. He couldn't swallow a drop of spit if his life depended on it.

"If they start eatin' ice cream I'm just gonna fall down and die."

Finally, Larry spoke, "Let's make ice cream some other time. We got cookies to eat now."

The trauma had been too much for Terry. "I gotta get another cookie," he whispered. "Ain't fair that I don't get none," he said, nibbling on the cookie he had hidden in his pocket.

His family hadn't discovered the two missing cookies, which was good, but they hadn't invited him down to eat even one with them, which was bad. As a matter of fact, it was pretty unusual. *Pa don't ever wait this long to forgive me,* he thought, squirming around with chewy cookie all over his teeth. He tossed his nickel onto his bed. *He should have called me down and forgiven me. That's the Christian thing to do.*

So he sat and sat, wondering how anybody could be so mean to torture a kid the way his father was. "Shoulda left with Railroad Jack and bought a nickel's worth of candy to live on. That would be a better life than this."

It sounded like a party downstairs. The more they laughed, the angrier Terry got. He fumed and nearly went out of his mind with visions of Mrs. Springer's cookies dancing in his head. *They're just pigs. Stuffin' cookies in their mouths downstairs. Into their cookie-eatin' mouths.*

Pa's havin' fun with them, but he never has time for me. I don't even get to go to the circus. Pa hates me. I know he does.

Larry smacked his lips so loud that Terry could hear him through the floorboards. *There's got to be a way to get just one 'fore they pig away all of 'em.* But how?

At first he was stumped, but then it came to him. All he had to do was create some distraction, some noise outside the house that would give him enough time to get down and snatch a couple of sweet, chewy cookies before the others caught him.

Rifling through his brother's desk, he found an old horseshoe and some twine. "This will do the trick," he whispered. Terry quickly tied a knot around the horseshoe and lowered it through the window down toward the front door. With a flick of his wrist he gave it enough momentum until it banged loudly against the door several times.

"Someone's at the door," Sherry shouted.

Terry yanked the horseshoe up and listened as her feet headed from the kitchen, through the hall and onto the porch.

"Who's there?" Rev. Youngun called out after her.

"No one's there, Pa."

"Are you sure?"

"Sure, I'm sure," she said, closing the door, but before she had made it back to the kitchen, Terry dropped the horseshoe and was knocking again.

Sherry went back out again. "You better come see, Pa," she said. "Might be that car burglar that Terry heard."

Terry listened as his father and brother headed toward the front porch. The moment they stepped outside Terry flew down the stairs, scurried into the kitchen, stuffed a cookie into his mouth and headed back toward the stairs.

Everything would have been fine if he hadn't gotten greedy for another. They were all still on the porch, and the cookies were still in the kitchen. It was another do or die decision, and swiping another cookie won out. Unfortunately he didn't know that his father had seen him.

Whatever indecision Rev. Youngun had felt about putting Terry to work on Reece's farm was now gone. Rev. Youngun took a deep breath, knowing what he had to do. What his father would have done.

Can't be weak. Got to be firm. Can't let Terry go on getting away with everything.

He looked at Norma's picture on the wall, wishing his wife were there to help him. Closing his eyes, he focused on her memory, and for a moment he thought he caught a trace of her perfume in the air. Holding the memory and the false scent, he held it tight until the ache in his heart misted his eyes.

"Norma, I gotta do what I think is right," he said, thinking about what he was going to say to Farmer Reece. He tried not to hear Norma's voice in the air warning him to think carefully about what he was planning to do, warning him not to try to recreate his own childhood, that he needn't make the same mistakes as his own father.

Then a little voice, Terry's voice, called out in his mind, asking if he had time to toss a baseball. *I never have time. Never have time for anything except disciplining him.* He looked at the red ball that had rolled under the sofa and was now collecting dust.

Terry hid behind the clothes rack in his room. He'd stuffed the cookie into his mouth as fast as he could the moment he heard Sherry scream like the bear in Goldilocks that someone had been eating her cookies. Nibbling up the cookie crumbs off his shirt, Terry sat back, savoring each morsel. The sugar made him feel better, more positive. "Everythin's gonna be fine," he decided.

The sweet moment didn't last long. His father called him to come downstairs.

The minute Terry entered the living room he saw the look in his father's eyes. *I'm in for it now,* he thought.

"Did you take any cookies from the kitchen?" Rev. Youngun asked.

Terry shrugged, playing for time. "What do you mean?"

"You know perfectly well what I mean, Terry. Did you take any cookies?"

Terry looked at the walls, the ceiling, the floor, and back to the ceiling. His eyes traveled all over the room, looking at everything except his father's face. "Wanna go toss the ball some?" he asked, still stalling.

"Answer my question."

"But you never, ever toss the ball with me."

"Did you take any cookies?" Rev. Youngun repeated.

Terry shrugged and looked away.

"I know you did, I saw you."

"Sorry," Terry said meekly.

"I am going to see Farmer Reece tomorrow about putting you to work."

Terry puckered up his lips. "You're just joshing me, ain't ya, Pa?" Then Terry saw the look in his father's eyes. Rev. Youngun wasn't kidding. "Please don't do that, Pa. The circus is special to me. Don't make me miss it. I'll be good."

"You always say that."

"I mean it this time. I'll die if you make me pick carrots all summer," Terry whined.

"You won't die." Rev. Youngun was getting impatient.

"And I'll get sick lookin' at all the squishy worms that Wormy will show me."

"His name is Mr. Reece. Not Wormy. And I think working in the fields is good for a boy."

"Then find some other boy. This boy knows it ain't good for him."

"*Isn't* good," Rev. Youngun corrected.

"I knew you'd agree with me on that, Pa."

Rev. Youngun fluttered his lips. "I'll be taking you over there tomorrow."

Terry frowned. *Wish I'da left with that hobo. Wouldn't even have said good-bye. Railroad Jack don't gotta pick carrots.* "Please, Pa, I don't want to go work for that crazy man."

"He's not crazy."

"Is too!" Terry said. "He's got dead dogs that he feeds."

"He does not."

"I heard some of the kids who work there sayin' he talks to dead dogs."

Rev. Youngun waved his son's worries away with a flick of his wrist. "They were just pulling your leg."

"Anybody who talks to worms is crazy."

"Terry, I've tried everything I know to get you to change. Maybe a little hard work will make you see the light."

"And what if I die of heat stroke?" Terry exclaimed, feeling his forehead.

"You won't."

Terry half closed his eyes, as if he were feeling faint. "And what if I get poisoned from bein' 'round too many carrots, and he tries to have me stuffed?"

"You're acting silly again. There's nothing wrong with carrots."

Terry shook his head vigorously. "If I never, ever saw another carrot again it would be too darned soon for me."

Rev. Youngun took a deep breath and let it out slowly. "Go on upstairs now."

"I won't go," Terry said. "You can't make me pick carrots."

"Yes you will, if I tell you to."

Terry stomped his foot. "No, I won't. I know you'll change your mind."

"Don't hold your breath."

"I'll hold my breath until you change your mind," Terry said, glaring.

"Go ahead. It won't bother me."

Terry stood very still and took a deep, deep breath. Rev. Youngun just shook his head, pretending not to care. He went about his business, sorting through the papers on his desk.

Terry began turning pink.

His father gave him a you'll-be-sorry look.

Terry began to turn red like a barber pole.

"That's enough," Rev. Youngun said.

Terry turned blue. His veins were sticking out, and he felt light-headed. His ears tingled with sounds that weren't coming from any-where.

"That's enough, I said!"

The veins in Terry's forehead were sticking out as his eyes clouded over. He began weaving, like he was going to fall over, his eyes flickering white like two slices of hard-boiled egg.

"Enough!" Rev. Youngun exclaimed. He rushed over and shook the boy until the air exploded from his lungs. Terry fell down to his knees, half passed out and half acting to build up sympathy.

"Are you all right, son?" Rev. Youngun asked, feeling like he'd done something wrong.

"Need to rest, Pa."

"Here, lie on the sofa," Rev. Youngun said, lifting his son.

Terry fluttered his eyes. "Need some water," he whispered.

"I'll get it."

Terry watched his father walk out of the room, figuring that he was home safe and would be at the circus tomorrow.

Rev. Youngun brought back a glass. "Drink this," he said, cradling Terry's head.

"Thanks," Terry croaked.

"You shouldn't have done that to yourself."

"I'm sorry."

"Can I get you anything else?"

Terry decided to go for it all. "Got any more cookies?"

Rev. Youngun looked at his son's face, then at the picture of his late wife on the wall. *Norma, I wish you were here,* he thought.

"Terry, you're going to work for Farmer Reece tomorrow, and that's final."

"Please don't make me, Pa. I'll be good. You gotta believe me."

"Work is what you need," Rev. Youngun said, taking Terry's hand. "Son, prayer changes things. Pray with me for the things that matter."

Terry dutifully bowed his head and prayed silently for the things that mattered. That it would start raining cats and dogs and a flood would wash away Wormy's farm. That carrots would disappear. That

Sherry would get pulled under by the privy monster and that an angel would leave fifty pounds of rock candy under his pillow.

"Now Terry, don't you feel better?" his father asked.

Terry sighed deeply. "I will if my prayers are answered." He turned to leave and whispered, "I ain't all bad. I'm just a kid who ain't wanted 'round here." Then he scampered up the steps before his father could say anything.

While his father sat in silence, wondering what he was doing wrong, Terry opened his window and stared out at the horizon. In the distance a freight train echoed, calling his thoughts to Railroad Jack. He thought again about running away.

"I ain't never gonna work on no carrot farm. Maybe I should just see how far this lucky nickel will take me," he whispered, listening to the train whistle until it faded away.

12

Wormy

❖

Willard Reece, better known as Wormy, was one of those curious sort of coots that every town has either hidden away or tolerates in a bemused sort of way. Folks didn't know much about him except that he loved worms and had his three favorite dogs stuffed and mounted when they died. But with that knowledge they figured he was a ninny to be avoided.

Reece just liked having the dogs around. He patted their heads and talked to them like they were still living and breathing. Sometimes he just plain forgot that they weren't alive because they looked so lifelike, stuffed in their favorite positions. Old Sparky the black Lab lay in a curled-up sleeping position by the fireplace. Ranger, the mutt, was posed sniffing by the front door, and Gobbler, the fat hound, was in the kitchen waiting to be fed. Once Reece had even put some water down in front of Gobbler because the dog just looked so thirsty.

It wasn't hard to figure out how Reece got his nickname. The fifty-five-year-old gray-haired man loved worms. He was always talking about worms and usually had a few big, thick night crawlers in one of his pockets. Wormy figured he had about a million worms in his carrot fields, which accounted for his carrots being so big and juicy.

Most folks tolerated Reece, but no one made any social calls out to his farm because the stuffed dogs were creepy and people suspected that his carrot cookies were made with worms. And they were right. Reece actually made cookies with worms in them. His were the only cookies donated to the annual church bazaar that the kids wouldn't grab.

As a matter of fact, some said he kind of looked like a worm. He was skinny, sunken-chested, and had a goofy grin and a flat head. His hair was stringy and clumped together like a sack of worms. Wormy was always walking fast, talking to himself, holding worms up close to his bottle-thick glasses, and telling the world how valuable they were.

"'Bout time folks appreciated worms like this, right, Sparky?" he asked the stuffed dog as he held up his pet worm named Wiggler.

The worm was a giant among the lowly things, hanging loose from Wormy's fingers—all sixteen inches of him dangling in the air.

"Nothin' wrong with bein' a worm. Without worms, where would this ol' world be?"

Of course the worm couldn't talk back, but Wormy thought the worm answered him by wiggling around like it was dancing in the palm of his hand.

"Guess you deserve a treat." Reece grinned and took the worm into the kitchen. "Look who I got, Gobbler," he said, holding the worm in front of the stuffed fat dog who seemed to be waiting until eternity for his next meal. Reece placed Wiggler into a bowl and scooped in a couple of tablespoons of brown sugar. The worm wallowed happily in it until the bowl began looking like sugary goo.

The phone rang five times before Wormy realized that it was the phone and not the cicadas droning from the trees. It was Rev. Youngun.

"You callin' 'bout needin' some fishin' worms?" Wormy asked, making an effort to be sociable. It was hard to pay attention when his pet worm was having so much fun in the bowl of brown sugar.

After a minute or two of small-town pleasantries, Rev. Youngun asked, "You remember about two months ago when I talked to you about my boy coming to work during the carrot harvest season?"

"I think so," Wormy said slowly, "but it's gettin' late. Already got me a pack of local boys pickin' like there's no tomorrow."

Rev. Youngun paused, then asked, "Can you use one more hand?"

Wormy heard the plea in the man's voice. "I might could use me a big strong boy who knows how to follow directions."

"That's what I had in mind."

Wormy knew the Youngun kids and thought the big one would do just fine. "Guess I *could* use some extra help."

"I was hoping you could."

"Send Larry 'round in the morning and I'll start him on the road to life."

There was a pause on the line. "I was thinking about sending Terry," Rev. Youngun said.

There was another pause on the line. Wormy held the phone away from his ear as if it had bitten his hand. "Rev. Youngun, I'm not sure if I'm up to watchin' ol' Red. I watched him shoot spitballs like a wildcat in church last Sunday. Hit me in the neck with two."

"I'm sorry, Willard. I didn't know."

"You were up there jawbonin' a sermon. If you ask me, a kid like that don't look like he's ready, willin', or able to do farm work."

"But he can learn. The work will do him good."

"I can't be nursemaidin' no wild kid. I got a farm to run," Wormy said.

"He'll work hard, I promise you."

"From what I hear, that kid's got so much spunk it's comin' out his ears. Why don't you make him run a few miles and wear him out?"

"I'm asking as a favor."

"Is there somethin' you're not tellin' me, Reverend? Is ol' Red givin' you a hard time?"

Rev. Youngun confessed that he was having a hard time disciplining Terry. Wormy had sympathy for the widower, but he also knew that Terry Youngun was no average kid.

"What kinda things you two do together?" Wormy asked.

"Things? What do you mean?"

"Things. You know, hunt, fish, them sort of things."

"I've been pretty busy lately and . . ."

"So you want me to work some sense into him, is that it?"

"I guess that's what I'm asking."

"Are you expectin' me to be payin' him?"

Rev. Youngun thought for a moment. He had always extolled the virtue of work and its rewards. If Terry didn't get paid for his labor, then it might affect his attitude about work for the rest of his life.

"How about you tell him you're paying him, and I'll reimburse you for what you give him."

Wormy knew that Rev. Youngun had a bank account about the size of a worm's brain. He also didn't think it was good to be telling white lies.

"How about I pay him for what I think he's worth. If he ain't worth a . . . er . . . darn, then I'll pay him nothin'. If the boy does a good job, then I'll pay him a normal kid's wage of twenty-five cents a day. How's that sound?"

"That sounds fine. I'll bring him by tomorrow morning."

After he hung up, Wormy patted Gobbler on the head and looked at the brown-sugar worm in the bowl. "Tryin' to get that kid to work will be like trainin' a mountain lion to use a cat box. Gotta keep a close eye on him tomorrow."

He puttered about the kitchen. "Hope that boy likes to eat carrots," he said, washing off a fresh bunch and putting them into the bottom of the icebox. He went out for a walk to think about things and called for Ranger to follow him. The stuffed dog didn't move.

13

Sideshow

❖

Jo-Jo sat on his stool trying not to look at the sideshow gawkers. Cringing faces. Frightened eyes. Women and children turned away in fear and disgust, unable to stare him down.

The shame and the agony had long since been replaced by a desperate loneliness in Jo-Jo. He was always alone except when a crowd was taunting him. His was a hurtful world with no hearts or flowers.

"You a wolf?" a teenager jeered, trying to impress his friends.

Jo-Jo turned his face toward the wall.

"Hey you, ugly boy, are you a wolf or a dog?"

"Come on, Billy, let's go," one of his friends said.

"No, we paid to see freaks and he's one of 'em. Ain't you, were-wolf?" the boy asked, snarling and biting the air, trying to act like a werewolf.

Jo-Jo did his best to think of pleasant thoughts. It wasn't easy because the boy wouldn't let up.

Picking up a stick, Billy stuck it into Jo-Jo's face. "I'm talkin' to you. You speak English?"

Jo-Jo was silent.

"You a deaf freak?" the boy taunted.

Jo-Jo slowed his breathing to keep himself calm. It was a trick that he'd learned from the other performers to help him endure the indignities. Then he felt the spit hit his face. A thick glob of it matted in the hair on his nose and cheek.

Wiping it away on his sleeve, Jo-Jo turned his eyes toward the boy, then jumped to his feet, growling loudly, shaking the bars on his cage. The kids ran screaming from the tent, leaving Jo-Jo to wait for the next group to come in and laugh at him. He didn't see Mr. Gomez watching sadly from the back of the tent.

Cole folded up the map of Mansfield and put it back in his desk as he turned up the lamp. He shined his silver ring on his pant leg, then took another piece of candy to suck on, thinking about the fast-talking hobo whom he had seen taking nickels from the crowd. He glanced at Jo-Jo who had entered his wagon after finishing his show, then turned his head away so as to avoid making eye contact.

Cole knew he should be nice to the boy because he would need him in Mexico. He needed Jo-Jo's knowledge of Spanish, but there was something about the way the boy looked at him that bothered him. It was the eyes—Jo-Jo's all-knowing eyes. Like he was reading Cole's mind.

Cole needed Jo-Jo for his plan, but he still kept his distance, like he was dealing with a wild animal who would bite at his throat any moment.

Jo-Jo's dark brown eyes froze on Cole's face. Then, without thinking, he bared his teeth the way he did on stage.

"Don't go trying to bite the hand that feeds you or I might not take you with me to Mexico," Cole sneered, forcing himself to make eye contact.

Jo-Jo slowly closed his mouth. "Mexico?" he whispered, suddenly feeling weak.

"Yeah, Mexico. But it's a secret. You let out the word to anyone, and I'll sell you to an Eskimo who'll have you pulling a dogsled."

"You're taking me back to Mexico?"

"That's right. I've been feelin' sorry for you, so I'm takin' you home," Cole lied.

It was a lie that Jo-Jo desperately wanted to believe. *Maybe my angel is watching out for me after all*, he told himself as he left Cole's wagon. Maybe he could believe again that his angel star was really up there.

Jo-Jo had to sit down outside on the wagon's steps to catch his breath. Mexico. The land of his birth. It was what he dreamed about:

going back to Guadalajara, living by himself in the hills. His mind was alive with *mariachi* music, tortillas, and sweet Spanish.

Maybe he's just doing this to hurt me. To trick me, he worried.

Not caring that he wasn't wearing his hood, Jo-Jo pushed the hair away from his eyes, nodding to Roger, Cole's tall, muscular driver.

"What kind of mood's he in?" Roger asked.

Jo-Jo shrugged, not answering, because he didn't trust the man. He wanted to ask if it were true about Mexico, because Roger would know, but Jo-Jo held back. *He's too close to Cole. Thick as thieves they are. He'll tell him I'm talking too much.*

Roger was cleaning off his ticket-taker uniform, which had been ironed so often that it shone like slick waxed paper. "Is he in for the night?"

"I think so," Jo-Jo said, walking off. He looked back at Cole's wagon. Jo-Jo was commonsense smart. He knew that Cole was too cold-blooded, too brutal to change his ways. *Why is he tryin' to be nice to me? It doesn't seem like him.* "The man's a devil," Jo-Jo mumbled, slipping on his hood.

He stepped carefully through the knee-high weeds behind the wagons to where the other performers were sitting by the cooking fire drinking coffee and eating brown Betty pudding. All he could think about was going back to Mexico. Looking up, he scanned the night skies.

"I wish I could fly to Mexico," he whispered.

He didn't hear Alice the half lady come up behind him.

"Wouldn't it be wonderful if we had wings?" she said, closing her eyes at the happy thought.

Jo-Jo frowned. "Then Cole would have something else to attract crowds with."

"If I had wings I'd be long gone," she said wistfully. "I'd fly away and find a special place where I'd never be different again."

"I'd fly to Mexico and find a family . . . like the Gomezes," Jo-Jo whispered.

14

Privy Time

❖

Terry sat by himself in the three-holed privy that had the name "Old Faithful" painted over the door. It was his thinking place. Where he could just sit and reflect without anybody telling him what to do.

He liked to sit there and try to decide what he wanted to be if he ever grew up. Just the other morning he'd wrestled with being either a detective or a rodeo star. Now he was thinking about working on a worm farm—and felt sick to his stomach.

Pa don't care whether I live or die. Ain't right him sendin' me 'round to work for a crazy man who talks to dead dogs.

The last light of day had dropped beyond the ridge, but the heat still hung in the air. The sky seemed massed for rain that was probably falling in the next county. It was always a shade cooler inside the privy. Terry listened to the bullfrogs grump about the coming rain. A lightning bug floated in, flying in a jerking pattern to the song of the tired cicadas.

Bzzzz.

Terry looked around, watching the whirring wings of the mosquito come closer. "Shoulda never brought a lantern with me," he said. He swatted and missed the pesky mosquito that dive-bombed toward his behind.

"Get away from me!"

The mosquito flew to the ceiling and hid in the corner, avoiding the spiderwebs.

Bzzzz.

The mosquito landed on Terry's rear, which made him jump. "Get offa me!" he snapped, slapping the air.

Usually in the privy he rocked back and forth like he was riding a horse, shooting his finger gun, looking for outlaws. Tonight he was quiet, not even worrying about the thunderclouds and heat lightning that had lit up the ridges. He had eavesdropped on his father's call to Farmer Reece and knew that tomorrow was going to be the worst day of his life. There had to be a way to get his pa to change his mind, but Terry didn't know where to start.

"He won't listen. He never does," Terry grumbled. "Adults just give kids a half an ear anyway."

Bzzzz.

He watched the skeeter from the corner of his eye, knowing that it was flying in low circles, waiting for the chance to make a butt shot.

It was bad enough that he was being punished and wouldn't get a chance to see the circus show, but it was worse thinking about doing hard farm work, picking carrots for a man who kept worms in his pockets.

"I'm tired of his 'clean off your plate' speech each night," he said, mimicking his father's "children are starving" speech. "I'm tired of bein' told to be good . . . bein' told to read books . . . bein' told what to eat."

Terry hit his fist into his palm. *And he don't never have time for nothin' fun. I oughta drop that stupid nickel down the privy hole. It sure ain't lucky for me.*

"I wish I lived somewhere else," he moaned, his voice shaky. "Wish I was born to someone else. Had a different pa." He put his hands over his eyes and didn't see the mosquito moving closer. "All I wanna do is be myself. What's wrong with that?"

Bzzzz.

The mosquito circled closer.

"Wonder where Railroad Jack is? Shoulda runned off with him. I'd be livin' free right now." He picked up the stack of paper squares cut from the Montgomery Ward catalog and tossed them into the air. "Why's everybody pickin' on me?"

"Terry," his sister called out. "Wanna help feed Moo-Moo?"

"No. Feed her yourself."

Sherry rapped against the door. "You don't have to be so mean."

Terry took one of the corn cobs from the emergency basket and tossed it through the half-moon hole on the privy door. "Quit botherin' me!"

The thought of hard work was actually making him sick to his stomach. He saw himself stooped over, sweating, flies buzzing around his face, picking horrible carrots, knocking off manure-filled dirt clods and sticking the worthless food into a burlap carry sack.

"Pickin' and eatin' carrots oughta be against the law. And if Wormy tries to make me talk to stuffed dead dogs, I'll kick the stuffin' out of him."

He squinched his eyes shut, trying not to think about the skinny farmer and his worms. "He'll be watchin' me like a hawk to make sure I don't hurt any of his worms. That ain't no way to spend a summer vacation. A summer workin' ain't no summer at all."

Bzzzz.

The mosquito saw its chance and dove for the soft spot, catching Terry off guard when it dug for glory on his fanny. Terry levitated off the seat, flailing his arms in pain, looking very much like a squirming insect doing a bug dance.

"Oh no," he moaned, rubbing his bottom. He knew he was going to have a lump for sure.

As the rain started falling, Terry rushed toward the house, watching the thunderclouds roll across the Ozarks, lit up by the dancing lightning on the ridge in the distance. His head was full-up with worries about being punished. The only thing left for him to do was to run away. It was a hard thought to ponder as he took the creaky stairs two at a time.

15

Father's Duty

❖

Rev. Youngun watched three minutes tick away. He tried to finish the newspaper but couldn't. It was one of those reflective, woebegone moments when his heart hurt out of loneliness. Terry was on his mind. Dangit raised his hand and licked at Rev. Youngun's hand, which hung over the chair's arm.

Opening the curtains, Rev. Youngun watched the heat lightning dance across the hills, jagged in its brief electric flame. Each bright strike seemed to leave a momentary signature in the air. A few large raindrops fell with a thunderclap, then stopped. Everything was calm and silent, eerily so.

He looked at the picture of his late wife, Norma. Her voice seemed to linger in his mind. *Thomas, every child is a compromise of nature. They can't always be the way we want them to be.*

He looked out at Miss Beedlebottom's car, thankful that it was still in one piece. *I wonder how I can tell her what happened? Maybe I should just get the gas pedal fixed and not mention what happened.*

He saw himself waiting in her high-ceilinged, ostentatiously furnished house. Sitting on the overstuffed sofa, feet planted on the expensive old rugs, he would be waiting like a child for his punishment. Waiting for the older lady with high cheekbones and translucent skin to walk in, fingering the expensive cameo brooch that hung from her collar. She would be holding a cupped hand behind her ear to hear his explanation about why the gas pedal on her expensive car was broken. About why she shouldn't cut off her annual donation to the church.

The jangling of the phone broke his mood. Rev. Youngun caught it on the third ring, looking out the window at the fireflies dancing toward the moon. It was Maurice on the other end.

"Just wanted to make sure you'd have the kids ready in the mornin'."

"They'll both be dressed and fed when you get here."

Maurice hesitated, then asked, "What about Terry?"

"I'm not going to let him go. I can't. He's taken things too far this time."

"Sherry told me. He's a good boy, Reverend. Heck, all boys cause trouble at some time or another. Terry's just a boy who was born a runt and thinks he's Hercules."

"Maurice, Terry needs to learn there are limits to my patience."

"Just cut him some slack, and let me work on him for a few days. Then maybe we can all go off fishin' together." Maurice let his words hang in the air.

Rev. Youngun said flatly, "I don't have time."

"Why don't you just make the time and take him to the circus?"

"I can't. I already told him he's not going."

"You *can*," Maurice said, frustration coming through in his voice. "There's nowhere in any book that says a daddy can't change his mind. The circus only comes once a year. It was the biggest thing in my life when I was a pup."

"No, Maurice, I have to follow through on what I said."

"Will you at least think 'bout it? Maybe let him go but don't let him buy no candy?"

"No," Rev. Youngun said, wanting to end the conversation. "He's starting work tomorrow at Reece's."

Maurice paused. "You really think Wormy's gonna get a day's work outta a boy who ain't never put in a full day's work in his life?"

"Then it's time he learned."

"And you think it's good to have him workin' 'round that worm man? I've heard he's a bit dinged in the head."

"That's just rumor."

"And some rumors is true. With all due respect, I think you ought to change your mind."

"Good night, Maurice," Rev. Youngun said, wishing he hadn't picked up the phone.

❖ ❖ ❖

It was not to be a good night for sleeping. The crackling lightning bolts and the threat of rain kept the town on edge, turning crisp white sheets into sticky blankets. Terry lay in bed with a wounded, sinking notion that life was about to end. His hair was wet with sweat. He wanted to cry.

Life was hard to understand. It seemed that everything Terry did was wrong, bad, and worse. He rubbed his lucky nickel, wishing for happy times, but only sad thoughts came. He hardly slept a wink, and when he did, he dreamed of picking ten-foot carrots all covered with worms. He dreamed of a crazy man running through the woods with dead dogs howling behind him. Terry wished that tomorrow he could be going to anyplace on earth—even school—except going to pick carrots for Wormy Reece.

Running away was the only answer.

16

Grouchy

❖

Terry awoke so grouchy that Sherry kept two steps behind him as they went down the stairs to breakfast. His father had a brown bag of cereal ready for them at the table.

"I ain't gonna eat rocks for breakfast," Terry declared.

"They're not rocks. It's a healthy cereal."

"What'd you eat?"

Rev. Youngun shrugged. "Just coffee and an apple."

"That's what I'll have."

Larry looked at his brother. "You want a cup of coffee?"

"Better than these rocks," Terry said, pinching a wad of the hard cereal between his fingers. "I'll save this stuff for my slingshot." Under his breath he mumbled, "Hope you all get the runs."

"What did you say?" his father demanded.

Terry shrugged. "Just said I hope you all have fun. You know, at the circus."

Terry grumped for the rest of the breakfast, feeling hurt and left out as they talked about the circus. He wanted to go worse than they could ever imagine, but he didn't let on, pretending not to care.

"Want me to bring you some popcorn?" Larry asked.

"Nope. Pa's sellin' me to Wormy Reece as a field hand."

"I'm not selling you."

"Might as well. Ain't right sendin' your boy to go pick worms and stupid carrots in the hot sun." He looked at the three of them. "Just make sure you put the words, 'He Shoulda Runned Away,' on it."

"On what?" his father asked, taking the bait.

"On my tombstone."

"You're not gonna die." Larry smirked. "Lots of kids work in the fields."

"I ain't like lots of kids. They don't gots a heart condition like I do."

"Whatever on earth are you talking about?" his father asked.

"Didn't wanna have to tell you, Pa, but Dr. George said I had a bad ticker."

"He did?"

Terry nodded. "When I was there havin' my fever checked. He whispered to me that I had a bad ticker that couldn't be fixed." Terry put his hand on his forehead, then slowly lowered it to the table like he was fainting. "Think I'm havin' a heart spell right now."

Larry, Sherry, and Rev. Youngun looked at each other with what's-he-up-to-now looks on their faces.

"Terry," his father said, "I'm going to call Dr. George immediately. But if you're lying to me, you'll work every weekend for Mr. Reece through the winter."

Larry looked at Terry. Sherry looked at Terry. Terry kept a passive look on his face. "I'm tellin' the truth. That's what he said. Seems you ought to be more concerned about lettin' me go upstairs to rest than worryin' 'bout the words I heard."

"If you really have a heart condition, then of course you'll go right up to bed to rest."

"Ticker condition. He said I had a bad ticker that couldn't be fixed."

"Go upstairs and rest while I call him."

Then it dawned on Larry what Terry was talking about. "Is your watch still broken?"

Terry nodded without thinking. "My ticker's forever broke. You know that."

"Was Dr. George talking about your watch, son?" Rev. Youngun asked.

Terry nodded guiltily.

"And you wanted me to think it was your heart, didn't you?"

Terry nodded again.

"I'm disappointed in you. Trying to skirt the truth is dishonest."

Terry's lip started to quiver. He was desperate to get out of working. "I won't do it again. Please don't make me go to Wormy's. He might stuff me like he stuffed his dogs."

Rev. Youngun shook his head, ignoring Terry's comment. "Sometimes a boy needs to go where he doesn't want to go to realize what he shouldn't have done."

That's when Terry went for broke and began wailing. "Please, Pa," he sobbed, "don't make me go work in no worm field. I'm 'lergic to worms. They make me sick."

"Calm down, Terry."

"I'm a-fearin' that the worms are gonna crawl up my nose and suck out my brains. And I dreamed last night 'bout dead dogs howlin' at the moon, tryin' to eat my toes off. Please, Pa, let me go to the circus, and I'll be forever good."

It was quite a performance as Terry put on a powerful cry, falling to his knees, wringing his hands, wailing and throwing his arms in the air, and then falling flat on his back and kicking his legs back and forth like he was possessed. Larry and Terry thought their father was going to give in, but Rev. Youngun held his ground.

"Go feed Honker. See if you can do that without causing trouble. Just don't tease him."

"I won't, Pa."

When Mother Goose, Honker's mate, had died, the old, half blind male goose had adopted the Younguns' white mailbox as one of its own. Even though he nipped at anyone who got near his white mailbox—including the mailman—everyone tolerated Honker.

Though his father had told him otherwise, Terry had every intention of teasing the goose. With the bucket of goose feed in his hand, Terry skipped toward the mailbox. "Honker! Honker! Where are you?" he shouted, kicking a stone loose from the hard-packed earth.

"Here's your food," he said, pouring the dried corn on the ground. He looked around, knowing that any second, the big, tough white goose would charge at him, trying to nip him on the behind.

"Honker," he whispered, a nervous grin on his face. "Where are you, Honker?"

Terry hesitated, wondering if his father was watching. The fun was in seeing if you could touch the mailbox without getting nipped. "Ready or not," he whispered, then raced the last few steps to touch the white mailbox.

The old goose came out of the bushes honking and flapping its wings. *"HONK! HONK! HONK!"*

"No, Honker, no!" Terry shouted, jumping up into the air to keep the goose from nipping his rear.

"HONK! HONK! HONK!"

The old goose raced after Terry, stretching out its neck to get a good nip. Terry tucked in his behind as far as he could until it was practically touching his belly button. Running, jumping, sliding, dodging, he did everything he could, but the old, half blind goose finally nipped onto the back of his pants and clamped hard on an inch of his rear.

"Ouch!" Terry laughed, jumping around and trying to shake the goose loose, but the goose hung on, flapping its wings, holding on to Terry's behind like it was a real treat.

"Let go, Honker!" Terry screamed, spinning around, feathers flying. The goose wouldn't let go.

"Terry!" his father shouted from the porch. "Quit teasing Honker!"

"He's tryin' to eat me, Pa," Terry shouted, racing by the front porch with the goose hooked onto his britches.

"Stop it!" his father warned. "Take Honker back to the mailbox."

"Yes, Pa," Terry shouted, running back up the road with the goose clamped on his rear.

The old goose only let go of Terry's pants when he got back to the end of the driveway and scurried into the bushes.

Should I touch the box one more time? Terry wondered.

He backed up toward the box, wiggling his behind around, daring the goose to come get it. "Honker, here's what you want," he taunted. "Come take a bite."

When Terry was four feet from the box he spun around and raced to touch the mailbox, but the goose was ready for him. "Can't catch me." Terry laughed. Then he tripped.

The goose was all over him, nipping and pulling his rear like it was cotton candy. "Get off!" Terry screamed.

Inside the house, Rev. Youngun put the paper down. "What's that boy doing?" When he got to the top of the driveway he found Terry sitting on top of the mailbox.

"What are you doing up there?" Rev. Youngun asked.

Terry shrugged. "Just sittin'."

"Just sitting?" his father said. "You sure you're not teasing old Honker?"

Terry looked off down the road. "Thought I'd just wait up here for the mailman. That's all."

"Then you'd have a long wait. He doesn't deliver until tomorrow morning," Rev. Youngun said. "Let me help you down," he said, stepping forward, forgetting about the goose.

Terry looked at his father, then at the bushes, but he didn't say anything. The moment his father picked him up, the goose came charging out to take a big nip.

"Stop that! No! Quit it!" Rev. Youngun said, wiggling around, trying to shake the goose off the back of his pants. The goose wouldn't let go. Rev. Youngun spun around and around in a whirl of dust and feathers. The goose finally dropped off, scurrying back into the bushes.

Terry couldn't stop laughing as they walked back to the house. "You're funny, Pa." Terry smiled as he opened the door.

"And you purposely went and teased that poor old goose. Now go upstairs and get your work shoes on. I'll take you over to Reece's farm after Maurice picks up Larry and Sherry."

Terry was stunned. He couldn't believe that his father wouldn't give in. Slowly, his feet dragging across the throw rug, he left the room. At the doorway he stopped and turned, his eyes red.

"One day you're gonna find me gone " he warned.

17

Off to Work

❖

Terry peeked out from the upstairs window to watch Larry and
Sherry climb up onto Maurice's wagon. He had his toes and
fingers crossed, and he heard Eulla Mae Springer trying to talk his
father into changing his mind or at least delay Terry's starting work for
a day so that he could go to the circus.

"Circus won't be back for 'nother year. Let him come with us.
Maurice has free tickets so it won't cost you a thing."

"I can't, Eulla Mae. I've given Terry too many chances in the past."

"How 'bout just this one time for me? I'll keep a close eye on him."

"He's starting work on Reece's farm today. It's the only way I know
to get his attention. Soon he'll be on his way to being a young man,
and if I don't change his ways now, it'll be too late."

Sherry came back up the stairs to get her hat. Terry pointed his finger
at her like a conjurer casting a spell and made up a poem:

"So you're goin' to the circus
Without poor Terry,
I hope a big spider
Bites the nose off ol' Sherry."

"That's not nice." Sherry frowned.

Terry shook his finger in her face. "I hope you have a terrible time,"
he said, slamming his door shut.

He watched in shock as they rode off down the long drive. "They're goin' to the circus without me. I can't believe it," he moaned. He threw the lucky nickel against the wall. "You ain't lucky!"

"Terry, time to go," his father called out.

It was one of those moments when Terry wished he could disappear—just blend in with the wallpaper and become invisible.

"Terry, it's time to go, I said."

"Time to go *die*," Terry said sarcastically, kicking the bedpost.

With his clumpy, church-donated two-sizes-too-big work boots on, Terry looked at himself in the mirror and suddenly felt very skinny, gawky, and out of place in the world. "Can hardly pick up my feet, let alone pull up heavy carrots," he complained. He clomped down the stairs, purposely making as much noise as he could to bother his father. He stood near the door, looking up at his father. "You still got time to change your mind."

"Nope."

"Please. Just take me to the circus, and I'll eat carrots every day until I die."

"No. Today you're going to learn to pick carrots."

Terry turned away, mumbling, "Rather pick my nose with a rake."

"What did you say?"

Terry kept on walking and called out over his shoulder, "I said I need to itch my nose for goodness sakes."

Rev Youngun just shook his head.

They rode in silence through the glare of the morning sun, which hung like a fireball on the horizon. The sky, bleached white, hung still, waiting for wind. Terry sat as far away from his father as he could without falling off the wagon seat. *Shoulda runned away. Shoulda followed Railroad Jack. I could probably be eatin' Tootsie Rolls and drinkin' Cokes on the top of a train. Headin' to live in some factory where they make cookies.*

"You got your lunch?" his father asked.

Terry nodded.

"You have your handkerchief?"

Terry nodded again.

"I'll come back and get you at sundown. You'll be ready for a warm bath and a good night's sleep by then."

"Be ready for the graveyard," was all Terry answered. "Probably won't have no toes left after them dead dogs get through with me."

"You'll be fine. Hard work never hurt anybody. I used to love it when I was your age."

"Then you can take my place. Shackle me to the bed, but don't make me pick carrots, Pa."

Rev. Youngun wanted to smile but kept his lips tight.

"Think I might call the sheriff," Terry mumbled.

"Why?"

"So's he'll arrest you for sendin' a little kid to a crazy man's farm. Bet he's a crazy witch."

Rev. Youngun was frustrated. "Mr. Reece isn't crazy."

"He don't row with both oars. Talkin' to dead dogs ain't normal. That's what they say he does."

"Who says?"

Terry nodded like he was telling the gospel truth. "Heard some men talkin' in town."

"Well, you shouldn't be listening to other people's conversations."

Terry raised his hand like he was in school. "What happens if a cougar comes chargin' out of the woods and grabs me by the britches and eats my butt off?"

"That won't happen."

"Or what if an eagle comes and claws my eyes out?"

"You're just being foolish."

"You'll think it's foolish when I come back without any eyeballs and my behind bit off by a rabid cougar."

"I'm not going to talk about it."

"That's 'cause you won't care if that crazy man stuffs me like them dead dogs of his." Terry pouted.

"I'm tired of your shenanigans," said Rev. Youngun.

When they got to Reece's farm, Terry looked across the carrot patch at the other boys who were picking carrots and loading boxes. The heat hung low over the fields. To Terry the boys looked miserable. *Gonna die pickin' carrots. I know I am.*

Farmer Reece came over, wondering what he was going to do with a boy who was known as the redheaded wild man of Mansfield.

"Morning, Willard," Rev. Youngun smiled. "I see you have a good group of boys working."

"That I do," Reece said, his face a seam of sun-dried wrinkles. His cheekbones jutted out from his rawboned face, stretched back over his smile. Reece reached up and shook hands with his neighbor, then looked at Terry. "And I hear that you want to be one of them, son."

"Then you heard wrong," Terry said, bending down and pretending to fix his boot.

Reece looked at Rev. Youngun. "He doesn't seem happy about this."

Rev. Youngun looked at his son. "He just needs to learn the virtue of hard work."

"There's no virtue in hard work," Terry mumbled. "Just sweat and itchy underpants."

Reece shrugged. "Well, son, I guess I'm gonna have to learn you that virtue then." He reached up and lifted Terry down from the wagon seat. "You got your lunch?"

"Yes."

"Yes, sir," his father corrected.

"Yes, sir, Wormy sir," Terry mumbled.

"No, Terry, it's Mr. Reece," his father corrected.

"Sorry," Terry shrugged, looking away.

"Good. And here's what I have for you," Reece said, taking a thirteen-inch worm from his pocket. "All my workers get to have their own pet worm. And name them too." Terry looked at the slimy, wiggling thing. "What you gonna call your worm, Terry?" Reece asked kindly.

Terry looked at the long, slimy, wiggly thing. "Gonna call him, FB."

"FB?"

"Yeah, Fish Bait."

Rev. Youngun looked away, hoping that Reece wouldn't change his mind about letting Terry work for him.

Reece wasn't pleased. "Well, Mr. Terry Youngun, I see you're intent on makin' yourself miserable. You just go on over there and grab a burlap sack and start pickin' carrots like them other boys are doin' over there by the pond."

"But I don't know how."

"Ain't nothin' to it," Reece said, putting his hand on Terry's shoulder. "Just pick 'em and knock the dirt clods off and stick 'em in the sack."

"Where you got your dogs hid?" Terry asked.

"What'd you say?"

"Where you got your dead dogs?"

"Dead dogs? What are you talking about?" Reece asked.

"You know," Terry said, eyeing the man coldly, "the ones you had stuffed."

Reece grinned broadly. "Oh, I've got three inside the house."

"See, Pa," Terry said.

"Good-bye, son," Rev. Youngun said, clicking the reins. "I'll be at the church if you need me."

Terry let him ride off without saying anything. *Pa don't care if I live or die. Got to take care of myself.* He had a fail-safe plan for getting out of work. A plan that would give him time to stall and come up with an escape plan. When his father was out of earshot, he turned to Reece and asked, "You got a privy 'round here?"

Reece shook his head. "Not out here in the field. Boys just go over in them woods and hoe out a drop hole with their boots. Plenty of good leaves over there."

"Leaves! Don't you got no cobs or cut-up magazines?"

"Just use the leaves." Reece pushed Terry out toward the field. "Now you get goin' and pick lots of carrots."

"You really got stuffed dogs?"

"Sure. Three of 'em. Better than photographs."

"Why'd you have 'em stuffed?"

"'Cause I like havin' 'em around. Now scoot. I'm payin' you by the day so get goin'."

When Terry was five steps away, Reece called out, "Be nice to your worm."

"Don't worry 'bout that." *I'll be nice all right—until I get my fishin' line,* Terry thought.

"Remember, only pick the good carrots," Reece called after him.

"No such thing as good carrots," Terry mumbled.

At the edge of the pond he saw a fish break the surface. He reached into his pocket and took out the worm. "Nice knowin' you," he said, as he tossed it into the water.

18

Hobo Greenbacks

❖

Cole and Roger went through their checklist for the day, making sure that everything was in order. Each performer was fed, their dirty clothes washed, and any special needs attended to. Cole had an investment in each performer, so it was in his best interest to keep them all healthy.

When he got to Jo-Jo's wagon, he found it empty. "Where'd Jo-Jo go?" Cole asked.

Paul, the midget, pointed off toward the roadie camp. "He just went for a stroll over to the roadies' camp."

"He didn't get permission," Cole fumed, storming off.

He found Jo-Jo eating breakfast with the Gomez family, laughing over a joke in Spanish. The boy wasn't wearing his hood.

Cole was furious. "Jo-Jo, what are you doing over here, givin' everyone a free peek at your face?"

The Mexican family fell silent, looking away. "We were just talking," Jo-Jo whispered. Without his hood he felt vulnerable. He put it back on.

Mr. Gomez stood up and explained that they had invited Jo-Jo to have breakfast with them. "It's not the boy's fault. There was no harm done."

"I don't need you gettin' one of my freaks thinkin' he's normal." Cole lifted Jo-Jo up by the collar. "He'll never be normal. That's why people pay to look at him. 'Cause he's a freak."

Jo-Jo struggled to break Cole's grasp, then, seeing that it was hopeless, went limp. It looked like Cole was holding a hairy rag doll.

"I own Jo-Jo, do you understand that?" Cole said to Mr. Gomez. "I don't want you people talkin' with Jo-Jo no more, or I'll have you fired."

Jo-Jo looked at the Gomez family, his haunting eyes speaking without saying a word. "Good-bye," he mouthed, his pink lips slowly forming the syllables, as Cole dragged him away.

Mr. Gomez hugged his family together, saying that they should all pray for Jo-Jo and the angel star he had told them about. "Pray that Jo-Jo can find his angel star and be happy."

"But he could be happy with us," his oldest daughter whispered.

"Cole will never let him go," Mr. Gomez said sadly.

Cole put Jo-Jo back into his wagon, then took a morning stroll through Mansfield, going over the last-minute details of his plan. He wanted to case the bank and walk through the path one more time. It was a shade cooler than the day before, but from the way the sun was drying up the morning dew, he knew a scorcher was coming. Walking the route he planned to follow later, he timed how long it would take for him to run out of the back door of the bank, down the alley and across the field, and make it back to the circus before the last freak show was over.

Shouldn't take me no longer than five minutes. There will be all kinds of confusion goin' on in the bank. With me bein' disguised as a hobo, the law will be headin' toward the hobo camp, not comin' to the circus.

The way he figured it, with Stein putting the circus receipts there for safekeeping, and the money the merchants must have deposited with all the visitors coming to town, there would be close to twenty thousand dollars in the vault. And that wasn't even counting the money the bank kept on hand for everyday business.

Twenty thousand dollars will pay off my debt and leave me ten grand in travelin' money to make it to Mexico. Then it dawned on him. How was he going to walk into Stein's office out of the blue and pay off his debt in cash with everyone in town knowing that the bank had just been robbed?

Don't think he'll believe I saved it up. And with the bank probably goin' to offer a reward, that ol' Mr. Stein will figure I pulled the bank job, turn me in, get the reward, and then keep my sideshow. Cole shook his head. *Nope, can't do that. Guess I'll just have to slip away when we pull up stakes and head off.*

Cole knew that Mr. Stein would send someone after him to collect the debt, but he figured that he and his show would be long across the Mexican border before they ever figured out where he had headed.

My freaks can use the rest. I'll tell 'em they all get a nice vacation. They'll never figure where I'm takin' 'em.

Before he went back to the circus, Cole went down to the train tracks to where the hobo camp was. The air was hung with a sickly sweet smell—a mixture of rank food, stale cigarettes, and homemade wine. Cole knew the sour smell of poor men and hard times. He'd grown up with it.

"Any you boys want some work?" he asked.

Listless eyes sunk in weathered faces flickered alive. Some were ill, looking older than their years. Others had the shrunken physiques of bad eating and hard drinking. Those that weren't too hung over to answer shuffled over toward him.

"What you got in mind?" a lanky, string-bean-looking hobo asked.

"Just some pickup work. Light trash. Nothin' more than that."

"How many men can you use?" a hobo asked with a Spanish accent.

"Ten, twelve. Just meet me at the town square across from the bank at three o'clock."

"What you payin'?"

"Twenty-five cents an hour. Those that work hard, I'll give a full day's work tomorrow." Cole reached into his pocket and took out a wad of dollar bills. "Here, I'll give each of you a buck in advance. How's that sound?"

Hoboes who had no intention of working suddenly acted like they were serious heavy loaders and moved faster than they had in years to get in line for their dollar. Like hungry animals, they jostled to get their share. Cole knew that most of them wouldn't show, but all he needed was four or five hanging around the bank, and he'd be home free.

As he walked back toward the circus, he grinned. *No one trusts a hobo. They're natural-born thieves.*

Railroad Jack and Skeeter returned to the camp moments after Cole left. "Where'd you boys get those hobo greenbacks?" Jack asked the crowd of happy-faced men.

"Man just handin' 'em out. Said it was a down payment on our comin' to work for him later."

"A man just gave away money? What was his name?"

"Stupid," a hobo said, giggling.

The hoboes nodded. The biggest one chuckled. "Since I only wanted to work for four hours and he was payin' twenty-five cents an hour, I figured I already put in my four hours and don't need to work no more." The other hoboes nodded their agreement. "So what say we all go to that saloon and see if our money's good?" one of them asked.

As they walked away, Jack grumbled, "Wish we had gotten some of those hobo greenbacks. I'm kinda hungry. How 'bout you?"

"I'm hungry if that's what you're askin'. Sure could use a hot plate of . . ."

"Don't say it," Jack shook his head.

"But I'm just hungry for beans. Can't help it."

"Hoboes are always hungry. But I got to earn some more nickels 'fore we can chow down again. And it won't be beans."

Skeeter's stomach grumbled as they walked along. "Sure wish we had some money."

"I'm broke."

Skeeter chuckled. "Man like you is never broke. Always savin' for an emergency."

As they passed the train station, Jack took out a ten-dollar bill from his shoe. Skeeter's eyebrows rose.

"Where'd you get that?"

"Been savin' it for an emergency. But I feel my luck's 'bout to change."

"What you gonna do with it?"

"Go to the bank, get it changed to two fives so I can put one back in my shoe. Then we'll go buy us some ham and eggs with red-eye gravy, biscuits, and hot, hot coffee."

"And some beans."

"No beans. You say that again, and I'm gonna find me 'nother travelin' buddy."

The teller didn't look happy to be dealing with two hoboes, and she didn't bother to hide her feelings. Jack didn't let her rude manners bother him and introduced himself with a flourish.

Seeing her nameplate, he said, "My name's Jack, Railroad Jack, the genius hobo."

"Can't imagine a genius being a hobo," the teller sniffed, holding his ten-dollar bill away from her body like it was diseased.

"I'm so smart I don't have to pay to live. People pay me." He took the two fives she held out. "Appreciate it, Miss Stevens," he winked, giving her a slight bow.

"You want to join us for dinner?" Jack winked again.

She huffed and began shuffling papers. He sat down on the floor, removed his shoe and folded up a five. As he and Skeeter left the bank, Jack ignored Mr. Givens, the bank manager, who was sitting in his office, eyeing them.

Givens walked over to the teller's cage, shaking his head. "I think we should post a 'No Hoboes Allowed' sign on the front door, don't you, Miss Stevens?" He looked outside and saw the group of hoboes holding dollar bills, standing in line at the saloon.

"Hope the sheriff is keepin' an eye on that riffraff. Especially that smart one who just said his name was Railroad Jack " Miss Stevens replied.

Back at the sideshow camp, Mr. Gomez crept alongside of Jo-Jo's wagon, hoping that Cole or Roger wouldn't see him. "Jo-Jo, can you hear me?" he whispered.

"Yes," the boy said quietly.

"We want you to leave with us. Come back to Mexico with us."

Jo-Jo said nothing. *Mexico. They want me to leave with them.*

"Did you hear me, Jo-Jo?"

"Please don't leave," Jo-Jo whispered.

"We have to. It's time we returned to Mexico."

"I don't want you to go."

"We want you to come with us."

"Mr. Cole will never let me go," Jo-Jo finally said.

"Then come with us anyway. No one has to know. We will sneak you away."

"He would come find me. Cole will never let me leave until I die. Good-bye, Mr. Gomez. I will miss you."

Cotton-Pickin'
Carrot Picker

❖

Terry walked across the carrot field feeling like he was heading to his own execution. For the first time in his life he truly regretted something he had done, but it was too late. Now, as he walked across a sea of the food he hated most in his life, Terry felt like he was walking the plank.

He hated work. He hated to sweat unless it was from serious playing. Looking around at the dozen lean, sunburned boys hunched over, straining under the pounds of carrots in the sacks on their backs, Terry felt like a trapped rat with no cheese.

One of the bigger boys with shoulders as wide as a wagon, wearing a sweaty, dirty hand-me-down shirt, looked up at Terry and chuckled. "We got ourselves a new fish."

"I'm no fish," Terry said.

"How's your worm?" the boy sneered, wiping back blisters of grimy sweat from his face.

"I let mine take a swim."

"You what?"

"Nothin'. I need a sack," Terry mumbled.

"You ever bagged carrots before?"

Terry shook his head.

"You ever done farm work before?"

"A little. For Mr. Springer. I need a sack."

The boy laughed. "You don't look happy. Guess you don't know how lucky you are to have this job."

"Lucky? I hate carrots, I hate worms, and I hate work."

"Quit your bellyachin'," the boy said, shaking his head.

Terry made a face. "I ain't bellyachin'."

"You better work hard or he'll stuff you like them dogs of his."

Terry's eyes went wide. "You seen them dogs?"

"Three of 'em. In the house. Lookin' like they's just waitin' to go for a walk."

Terry shivered, wanting to believe the boy was just joshing him. "Why'd he stuff 'em? What good are dead dogs?"

"Ask him."

"Already did. Where's the sack?"

The boy pointed to a pile on the back of the carrot wagon stacked high with filled boxes. "You sure aren't the friendly type. My name's Ronald. What's yours?"

"My name's Terry, but I won't be 'round here long 'nough for you to remember it," he said, walking over to the wagon to get a sack. His steps through the dirt left little dust puffs trailing behind him.

"Somebody might learn you a smart-mouth lesson," the boy called after him, gritting his teeth like he'd found sand in his gum.

Terry made a doodle sign with his finger on his nose.

"Think you got some sand in your gut, don't you, Red?"

Terry ignored the remark and kept walking. He heard the behind-his-back giggles and smirks but kept his composure. He didn't care what these boys said about him.

"You got anythin' else to say, Red?"

"Go bark up your own tree. You can stuff your nose with worms for all I care."

"Big talk from a little squirt." The boy started toward him, then stopped. "You ain't got enough meat on your bones to feed a starved mosquito."

There was another, smaller boy standing by the wagon. "Why you smart-mouthin' him?" he asked Terry.

"Just don't want to be here," Terry said, looking away.

"Best get used to bein' a carrot picker. Ain't got much choice, it looks like."

Terry shook his head. "I ain't never gonna be no cotton-pickin' carrot picker. Rather die than spend my summer workin' here for a man that's crazy as a loon."

A freckle-faced kid walked up to grab another sack. "Just don't eat the cookies if Wormy brings out any."

"Why not?"

"You never know what he puts in 'em. And don't go inside the house. Kid last week went in there and never came out."

"Yeah," the smaller boy whispered, "Wormy stuffed him."

"You won't catch me goin' in his house," Terry said.

"Then you better get to pickin' carrots. Word is if you don't pick enough, he picks you to eat worm cookies in his kitchen."

Terry hesitated. Picking up the sack was the final admission of defeat. *Need to escape*, he thought, looking around. There was no way out. The eyes and faces of the other boys, grinning like morons, blurred together. His heart was racing. His stomach ached with burning guts. He was sure he had a fever. He looked around for a privy, feeling like he would lose his breakfast. His belly juice was ready to shoot out. Then he remembered there wasn't a privy out there. *Don't wanna go dig a hole like a cat.*

With a gnawing in his stomach, he took a sack from the box and put it on his back. His fingers were trembling, and he felt lower than a snake's behind. He let out a deep sigh, fluttered his lips, then reached down and pulled up his first carrot.

"This ought to be against the law," he mumbled, knocking the dirt clods off. A big worm fell out onto his boots. Terry wished he could jump into a hole right then and there and pull the top closed.

"Gotta run away," he whispered to himself over and over as a tear raced down his cheek like quicksilver.

20

Simple Errand

❖

By the time Maurice, Eulla Mae, and the two Youngun kids reached Mansfield, the town was already crowded. Farmers, new immigrants, and traveling hucksters filled the streets, riding their wagons, buggies, and noisy automobiles.

Sherry was fascinated by the drawings and pictures on the circus posters that were tacked along the street. "Think they'll have any Indian riders this year?" she asked without taking her eyes off the poster.

"Nothin' there about it far as I can tell," Larry said.

"Can't wait to eat taffy and cotton candy and gumdrops and . . ."

"And you can't wait to get sick," Larry said dryly.

"Terry's gonna sure wish he'd been good," Maurice sighed. "That boy loves candy more than any child I've ever seen."

"Look at that poster!" Sherry exclaimed, pointing to a picture of Werewolf Boy.

Eulla Mae closed her eyes. "If'n I saw that thing at night I'd die from fright."

Before they could see it they smelled the chicken cooking and the popcorn. Sherry swore she could smell taffy and candy apples. When the peak of the circus tent appeared above the trees, they heard the clatter and rattle of the games and contests.

Outside the big top they saw roadies preparing for the day's show. "Look at that," Eulla Mae said in awe. "They've taken over Elderberry's entire field."

Maurice hitched the wagon, and they made their way through the mud, sawdust, and animal droppings, eyeballing everything. Bushels and bags of food and supplies were being delivered everywhere. The coppery smell of fresh meat hung near the cook stoves where briskets, ribs, and fresh-plucked chickens were being laid out.

A boy worked the crowds shouting, "St. Louie hot dogs with red Heinz ketchup. Get 'em while they're hot."

"That's where they sell the fried chicken!" Sherry shouted, pointing to the booth with the chickens painted on the side.

"Ought to call you Sherlock for figurin' that out," Maurice teased.

"Best food in the world is served at carnivals," Larry said, as if stating a well-known indisputable fact.

The pony ring was already taking customers, and there were six ponies eating from a pile of straw, waiting for the kids in line to pay their nickels. Nearby was the ring toss booth, the ball toss, and the fortune-teller's booth.

"I can smell the sizzlin' chicken livers," Maurice said, closing his eyes. "You kids are in for some eatin' treats."

Sherry went with Maurice and Eulla Mae to ride the ponies and play the games. Larry said he wanted to use the privy, but really he wanted to sneak around the performers' wagons, hoping to see a couple of stray freaks walking around.

He caught glimpses of a man without legs and a midget. An overstuffed woman was adjusting the garments of a woman with no arms. Between two wagons he saw a woman who looked like she had a chicken's head, so he moved closer for a better look.

"What you doin', boy?"

Larry turned to say something but went silent. The hair on the back of his neck went up. Standing behind him was a balding man in a starched-boiled shirt with a look of authority.

"You up to no good?" Adam Cole demanded.

"Ah, ah, no sir," Larry said. The man looked rough as an old cob and twice as dangerous.

"What you doin' peekin' around here then? Looking for a job?" Cole asked. "I could always use a good strong boy to help take down my show. Pays fifty cents an hour."

Larry whistled. "That's a lot of money."

"For a lot of hard work. You interested?"

"Have to ask my pa."

Cole smiled. "You shouldn't be so shy. Would you like to get a free look at the sideshow?"

Larry's eyes lit up. "You know some of the freaks?"

Cole laughed so loud it made Larry blink. "Know them? Why, I own them, son." He pointed to the name on the wagons. "Adam Cole's my name," he said, giving Larry a knuckle-popping handshake.

When his hand was freed, Larry asked, "You're Mr. Cole?" He flexed his fingers to see if they still worked.

"That's right," Cole said, moving closer. "Say, how 'bout I give you a quick look at the freaks then pay you fifty cents to run an errand for me?"

"To where?"

Cole reached into his pocket. "Just run these tickets over to the sheriff's office. Tell him that I want him and all his boys to come for the final show. Think you could do that for me?"

"And you'll pay me fifty cents?"

"And give you a free peek."

"Okay," Larry said, taking the tickets.

Cole handed him a dollar. "And if you take these extra tickets over to the general store next to the bank and the butcher shop on the other side of the bank and ask them to come to the show, you can have another fifty cents."

"A whole buck?"

"A *whole* buck." Cole pushed Larry toward town. "Now get going."

"What about my free peek?" Larry asked. He didn't hear Jo-Jo walk up behind him.

"Mr. Cole, you wanted to see me?"

"Jo-Jo, you want to growl for this boy?"

"No," the boy said, reaching to adjust his hood. But he wasn't wearing it and immediately felt uncomfortable.

"Say something to him, Jo-Jo," Cole said. He looked at Larry whose back was still turned. "Turn around, son, and meet a real werewolf."

Larry turned around slowly and caught his breath with a startled cry. He looked at the hairy-faced performer and went running off toward town to complete the errand. Jo-Jo watched sadly, wishing he too could be running free through town with the boy.

21

Escape from Wormy's

❖

After an hour of picking carrots under the brutal sun, Terry was ready to quit. His shirt was sopping wet, and his undies were sticking to him like flypaper. The way the other boys were watching him, Terry was convinced that Wormy had ratted to them about this being punishment work, and now they were all eyeballing him like jailers watching over an escape artist.

Standing out in the hot sun with a bag of carrots over his shoulder, the only thing between him and the other boys was more carrots. Wormy's wagon stood off by itself and didn't offer enough shade for a flea to take refuge in.

Reece rode through the fields, ladling out water from a jug on his horse. Terry gulped down two full cups. "You part camel or what there, Red?"

"Dyin' of thirst." Terry coughed, trying to catch his breath.

"How many carrots you picked?"

"Too many," Terry mumbled, not looking up.

"What'd you say?"

"Said two hundred or there 'bouts."

"That's good. Keep up that pace, and you might could earn a job workin' year 'round with me."

"Can't wait," Terry said sarcastically.

"And maybe later on, I'll take you up to the house and introduce you to my dogs."

Terry looked up. "I better keep workin'. Hard work's what I need."

"That's the attitude I like." Reece smiled as he rode away.

"I got to escape this loony bin. Everyone's nuts 'round here but me," Terry muttered.

The sunburned boys were all smiling, grinning at Wormy as if they were the luckiest kids on earth to be working at a carrot and worm farm.

I got to get free of this place. Got to get back home. But then what? His father would just drag him back to work some more. And Wormy would probably lock him in the crazy house. *No one will miss me. No one likes me. I'm better off running away.*

Finally, Terry told Mr. Reece that he had to go dig a hole in the woods and do his business. He walked quietly, pretending he really had to go bad. Once inside the bushes he ran like the devil was after him, cutting through the woods, across the fields, and along the road toward home.

Looking back and seeing no one, he laughed loudly. "Made it!" he shouted, as he ran head-on into the side of Reece's horse.

"Where you goin', Red?" Reece asked, looking at Terry sprawled out on the ground.

"Just needed to find a privy. Gotta go number two real bad."

Reece looked down from his horse. "I told you to use the woods."

"Don't wanna. Pa once told me 'bout a kid who used poison ivy to clean hisself and died from the rash."

"I see," Reece said. When Terry stood up, Reece reached down and pulled him up onto the horse.

"What you doin'?" Terry asked.

"I got a privy up behind the house."

"That's okay," Terry said, trying to squirm down.

"No, no, that's okay. Just don't tell the other boys."

They rode in silence up to the house. The field workers stopped and looked up, wondering where Reece was taking Terry. All Terry could think about was stuffed dogs, worm cookies, and monsters. *Bet he's got a fifty-foot worm in the basement. Bet he's got a bunch of stuffed dogs and cats, hangin' from the ceiling.*

After Terry had finished his business, he found Reece waiting outside the door. "Now, how 'bout you come and wait in the house. I'll just go check on the boys in the field, then you and I will have some lemonade and talk 'bout what's botherin' you."

Terry shook his head. "I better get back to work."

"No, your pa's worried 'nough 'bout you to send you over here to work. I just want to know what's goin' on.'

Despite his protests, Terry found himself pushed up to the front door. "Just go inside and wait in the kitchen," Reece said as he rode off.

Terry moved slowly. His sweat-dried shirt was uncomfortable. He opened the door and looked around. He didn't see Ranger the stuffed dog in the shadows. "Anybody home?" he whispered, chewing on his bottom lip. No answer. "Any stuffed bodies home?" he called out a little louder. Only the creak of the door answered him.

Against his better judgment, Terry stepped inside, just as a gust of wind came through the house and slammed the door shut behind him. "Oh, no," Terry whispered, suddenly wishing he'd behaved better in church. His ankle bones felt rubbery.

Then he saw Ranger. "Come here, boy," he whispered.

But the stuffed mutt didn't move. Terry's stomach did triple flip-flops.

"No," he whispered, while his mind said yes. The dog was stuffed. The rumors were true. He came very close to wetting his pants. Terry backed into the living room, and then he saw Sparky, the stuffed black Lab, lying by the fire. He stumbled into the kitchen and stepped on Gobbler, who was lying on the floor in front of a water bowl.

"Ahhhh!" Terry screamed, falling backward against the counter, knocking the gooey brown sugar bowl onto the floor. Wiggler the king-sized worm flopped around until Terry stepped on it, thinking it was a snake. It squished all over his shoe.

"Oh, geesh," he moaned, scraping his foot on the rung of the chair.

He spun around. Worm goo on the floor. A stuffed fat dog in the kitchen. Two other stuffed animals in the house. It was definitely time to vacate the house.

"No tellin' what this crazy man's gonna do to me," he said, breathing hard.

He looked out and saw Wormy riding toward the house. "I ain't gonna let him stuff me," he said, and ran out the back door.

Wormy saw the mess in his kitchen and his favorite worm squished all over the floor like a blob of brown jelly. He took off after Terry.

22

Running Away

❖

Wormy did his best to catch up with Terry, but he couldn't keep up with the twists and turns that Terry made. "Come back! You're supposed to be workin' for me!" he yelled.

"Ain't no way I'm goin' back," Terry mumbled, racing across the fields. Coming fast behind him, Wormy charged his horse through the brush, smashing the foliage.

"You stop right there!" Wormy shouted.

Terry ducked through low-hanging branches, under a fallen pine tree, past vines that whipped at his face and thorns that scratched him, pulling at his pants. He hopped over stumps and rocks, scaring up squirrels who raced up the trees. Birds lifted off in fright as Terry jumped, rolled, and staggered on, pulling the wild honeysuckle vines from his face.

On foot, there would have been no contest. Terry's young legs would have given him the edge. In the race against the horse, however, Terry couldn't last. He had to find a way to get ahead, so he ran blindly, as if he were in a slow-motion nightmare. His legs moved up and down like they were in a race with the devil.

Frogs croaked in anger as he sloshed through a mud pond, trying to keep from bogging down. He banged his head on a low branch and fought back tears, but his head throbbed, racked with sharp pain. At one point he was ankle-deep in stinky muck, but Terry wouldn't stop. Finding firmer ground, he pushed through gnarly vegetation, thick weeds, and brush, frantically looking for a place to hide.

"I'm comin' right behind you, Red," Wormy called out.

Terry slid down a bank and found himself in a place where the creek widened and filled the old trail. Wormy was coming fast, and Terry knew he didn't have time to wade chest deep through the cold water and then scramble up the muddy bank. He watched a water moccasin slowly swim across the surface until it disappeared into the weeds.

"Ain't goin' in there," Terry whispered, his legs trembling.

There was a fallen log over the creek not twenty feet away, so he clawed his way back up the bank and got to the tree.

"I see you, kid. You stop right there," Wormy commanded.

Terry looked back, then tested the tree with his foot. It was pretty shaky. "Ain't gonna pick no more carrots," he decided, and set out across the natural bridge. Halfway across he almost fell off, but the thought of picking carrots and holding worms helped him keep his balance.

Once across, he sat on the edge of the creek as Wormy rode up. "You better come back here," Wormy said.

"And you better go to the nuthouse."

"I'm gonna tell your pa."

"Tell him. I ain't comin' back."

"He's gonna tan your hide."

"He's gotta find me first."

Wormy reared his horse back. "You're in big trouble, boy. I saw what you did to my worm."

"I squished it all over the floor. Liked doin' it too. Now go kiss your dead dogs," Terry shouted, racing off toward the woods.

From the safety of the trees, Terry watched Wormy ride off. He knew that he was in a world of trouble. "What am I gonna do?" he moaned, wiping fresh sweat off his face.

He ran back along the familiar road feeling more confused than he'd ever been. His heart was pounding. Everything in his life seemed topsy-turvy. In his mind his father didn't love him. No one cared about him. Running away seemed to be the only way to change his life and teach everyone else a lesson. He decided to go home and get the things he would need.

When he got to the house, he hid behind the barn to make sure his father wasn't there. Looking down, he saw the mud clumps all over his shoes and pants so he pumped water on himself until he was cleaned

off. Then Terry walked across the barnyard toward the only place he'd
ever known as home.

Gonna run away forever, he told himself, his eyes misting with
soon-to-come tears.

Before he even opened the door, Terry was crying. In his mind, he
was in a box with nowhere to turn except to open the lid and jump out.

"Gotta do it. Gotta run away," he said, wiping his nose, trying to get
his courage up.

He paused in the hallway to look at the family pictures on the wall.
Pictures of his mother proudly holding him. Of his father and him
standing together on that Sunday after church when the traveling
photographer came by. Every picture was alive in his mind, calling him
to stop and think about what he was doing.

"He'll never miss me anyway," he said, looking away, knowing that
if he thought too long he'd change his mind.

Upstairs, Terry changed his pants, socks, and shoes, then took a
pillowcase and filled it with the things he'd need. A pair of socks. Two
pairs of underbritches. A shirt. The three remaining pieces of his
emergency candy stash.

Terry scribbled out a note to his brother:

I'll see you in ten yers. This is for you.

He put a piece of his precious candy on top of the note and left it on
Larry's bed. "I'm gonna miss him a lot," he said, taking a nibble of the
candy.

Stopping at the doorway, Terry walked back to find his lucky nickel
that he'd thrown against the wall. "Guess I'll take it with me. Might
need it to buy some food."

He looked in at his sister's room, wondering if he should steal the
rest of her candy. "She wouldn't understand," he decided, then turned
to go down the stairs.

Two steps down he stopped and went back up to her room. "Guess
I'll kinda miss her too," he said, leaving her one of his pieces of candy.
On a scrap of paper he wrote in big letters:

Sorry. I never hated you. I'll miss u for a few min-etts. Terry.

Looking at the candy he was giving her, he decided that she wouldn't know if he bit off a part. Leaving half, he chewed quickly, looking around her room, wondering if she had anything he needed.

"Girls don't got nothin' I need."

With only one piece of candy to travel on, Terry was wondering if he'd have enough energy to run past the mailbox, let alone run away for good. Though he knew he shouldn't, he took the sugar bowl from the pantry. That paled in comparison to running away anyway. "No turning back now," he whispered, placing the valuable energy bowl in the center of the pillowcase.

The hardest part was leaving a note for his father. Terry hated writing, and he sat at his father's desk agonizing over the words. Blank paper always scared the dickens out of him, but this was worse than school.

"At the rate I'm goin', he'll be home before I even write a word." He started, then scratched the words out. Then started and stopped three more times. Finally, the words came:

> Runned a-way four-ever. I will missss u more
> than u will miss me.
> Terry.

He thought about leaving the nickel on the note, then saw the red ball he and his father had once played catch with under the sofa and set it on the note.

Dangit sat in the corner watching him, wondering what the boy was up to. "Gonna miss you too, boy," Terry said, scratching the dog's head. As a good-bye present, he went to the kitchen and took out the chopped meat that was for dinner. "I'll just give you my share," he said. Before he was through he'd fed the entire dinner to the dog, who happily crawled under the sink and burped.

"You're welcome." Terry smiled.

With his pillow sack over his shoulder and the lucky nickel in his pocket, Terry was ready to go. Suddenly the phone rang. He hesitated, wondering if he should answer it. Lifting the receiver carefully off the wall, he put the phone to his ear. It was Wormy.

"Rev. Youngun," the man shouted over the crackling phone line.

"He's not here," Terry said, trying to disguise his voice.

"Where is he?"

"He moved away and ain't comin' back, so good-bye," Terry shouted, hanging up the phone. It started ringing within a minute but Terry ignored it.

He looked back over his shoulder as he walked away from the house. "Good-bye, house," he said.

He wanted to cry, needed to cry. "Wish they weren't makin' me do this," he moaned.

For a moment he thought about driving off in Miss Beedlebottom's car, but he only had a nickel, and he knew that wouldn't buy much gas. "Pa said it would take me to faraway places," he said, looking at the coin in his palm. "This ol' nickel ain't going anywhere far unless I get it there."

Crab Apple hee-hawed for Terry to come back, but it was too late. He walked along rubbing the nickel as fast as he could to keep from crying. His mouth was dry. Dust hung in the air, burning his eyes. A tear forced its way out, then another and another until Terry was crying so hard that the only thing he could think to do was squeeze the nickel with all his might. Honker came out but just looked at Terry, cocked his head, and let the sobbing boy pass.

When Terry got to the top of the hill, he looked back one last time. "My heart's in the right place. It is, Pa." Then he turned and looked off toward the horizon, suddenly seeing how big the world really was.

Show Time

❖

While Terry was running away, Maurice stood in line waiting for the show to begin. A thin-nosed, weary-looking man was keeping the crowd from going in. Maurice looked at the man's elephant-sized ears and weather vane nose and wondered if he was one of the freaks.

Everyone was wearing store-bought clothes and jostling, laughing, and talking about which freak they wanted to see. The boisterous, rambunctious crowd was ready to be entertained. Young peddlers, hawking magazines, dime novels, peanuts, and cigars cut in and out of the line. Scalawags and the town's best stood side by side, waiting for the tent show to open.

"It's gonna be real good. Real good," Maurice said, more to himself than to his wife or the Youngun kids.

"And you got those tickets for free?" Eulla Mae asked.

"For free. Just as I told you. The biggest toad in the puddle, the owner man hisself, stopped me in front of the bank and gave me the tickets."

"Adam Cole?"

"Adam Cole himself. Mr. Big Bug of the big bugs."

"If that don't beat the Dutch," Eulla Mae said, very impressed. "What was he like?"

Maurice was so excited to be going to the show that he forgot the rude treatment that Adam Cole had given him at first. "Nicest man you could ever hope to meet. Concerned about the town, about us watchin' out for the hoboes hangin' 'round."

Larry stood silently, wanting to tell the Springers about the money he'd earned from Mr. Cole by delivering tickets, but he didn't. Something about the errand had seemed sneaky. *But no harm done*, Larry thought. He decided to keep it to himself.

When they entered the gallery they walked past the clubfooted barker who was telling the crowd about the strange show that was about to start. The Springers and Younguns made their way to the front row.

"That man must have really liked you," Eulla Mae said to Maurice.

"Maybe I'll introduce you to him if I see him."

Maurice waved to the banker and the tellers, remembering how Cole had given them tickets also. He noticed a couple of deputies standing in the back of the tent. In the row behind him sat the clerks from several stores near the banks. One of the salesladies leaned over and thanked Larry for delivering her tickets.

"What was that about?" Maurice asked him.

Larry didn't want to lie, but he didn't want to ruin the show, which was about to begin. "Just did someone a favor," he mumbled.

Before Maurice could ask him for more details, the lantern lights were dimmed and the show began. Roger, Cole's tall, black driver, walked out and stared at the audience.

"Welcome to Adam Cole's world famous show of human oddities. No one is to touch the freaks unless we tell you to. And there's to be no smoking, spittin', or cursin' at these performers." He walked off, leaving the audience with an ominous warning of unspoken consequences if they broke the rules.

A baggy-eyed, heavyset, old carnie announcer strode out and began working the crowd to a fever pitch. "Folks, you're about to see a spectacular show. One of the most sensational—the most sensational—show on earth. Adam Cole has assembled a gallery of human oddities from all over the globe. From Europe, Africa, and Asia. He's traveled the world lookin' for these freaks of nature to exhibit for your pleasure. And here is the one and only, the world-famous, Mr. Adam Cole himself."

The crowd clapped and cheered as Cole walked out, resplendent in his white suit. "Thank you for coming," he said. "Everyone in the show really likes Mansfield and looks forward to coming back here. We've made a lot of friends," he said, walking out into the audience to shake Maurice's hand. "Thanks for coming," he said to Maurice.

"I . . . I wouldn't have missed it for anything," Maurice stammered.

Cole winked at Larry then reached back and shook the bank manager's hand. "Mr. Givens, I'm glad you and your staff could come. It's about time you closed the bank early."

"Didn't close it. Left two grumpy tellers who drew the unlucky straws."

"Tell them next year they'll have front row seats."

Cole worked the crowd, shaking the deputies' hands. Then, taking the stage stairs at a jump, he was back on stage, waving for the show to begin. He shook hands with the old carnie announcer who was dressed in an ill-fitted suit.

"Let's have a big hand for Mr. Adam Cole," the announcer shouted.

Cole waved to Maurice from the side of the stage, then went behind the curtain as the show began. The announcer droned on as he'd done in a hundred other small towns. "And right before your eyes is Alice the half lady. Born without arms. We've been trying to get her and Johnny the half boy to get married, to see if two halves make a whole, but they don't seem interested."

The crowd snickered, oblivious to the inhumanity and cruelty of the human exhibition. Johnny walked out on his hands, telling the audience how he had been born without legs.

Eulla Mae gasped, closing her eyes, swearing silently that she'd never let Maurice talk her into coming to this show again.

"Look at him, sugar bee," Maurice whispered, elbowing her side.

"No, don't wanna look."

Sherry was awestruck, hardly able to swallow the piece of hard candy in her throat. Squeezing onto Larry's arm, she wanted to close her eyes and not look at Ki-koo the bird woman who was flapping her arms and squawking, but curiosity kept her eyes open.

"Is that a real boy?" she asked, looking at Paul the midget who wasn't much bigger than a store-bought doll.

"He sure is. And so is he," Larry said, pointing to Sam the Alligator Man, who was announced as the newest addition to the show.

The announcer let Sam walk close to the crowd so they could touch his reptilian skin. Maurice tried to get Eulla Mae and Sherry to touch Sam, but they refused.

Adam Cole watched from the corner of the stage, timing the show. When Jo-Jo was announced to do his routine, Cole went back to his wagon to change for his own show.

❖ ❖ ❖

Jo-Jo was led onto the stage in chains and a collar. It was part of his stage act to act fierce, like a chained beast ready to burst loose and terrorize the audience.

Pretending to strain to get free, flailing his arms around, clawing at the air, Jo-Jo entertained the crowds. When the fake chains broke, the women in the audience screamed. Some ran or hid behind the men, who faked their bravery, hoping that the collar restraint on the werewolf would hold.

Larry watched, knowing that Jo-Jo was the same performer he'd just seen behind the wagons. The one he'd run from.

"Ain't you scared?" whispered Sherry, ready to bolt from the tent.

Larry didn't answer. He realized that the werewolf performance was just an act. That the hairy-faced person he'd run from was a boy who was acting for the crowd. The revelation, the knowledge, was both comforting and sad, because Larry now knew that Jo-Jo was a human being.

I'll never think of them as freaks again, he thought.

At that moment a hobo was slipping out of Adam Cole's wagon. But no one saw him.

Railroad Jack and Skeeter waited with the other hoboes across from the bank. Only six had come to earn more money. The rest had spent their dollar advance, which they'd figured they'd earned just for being alive.

The streets were filled with people streaming to the last circus show of the season. The festive crowd of strangers and town folks barely took notice of the hoboes. There were so many roadies and circus followers around that no one knew for sure who was who.

Jack tried to work the crowd, but no one would stop to ask him questions. They were all in a hurry to make the last show. "Can't even earn a wooden nickel," he grumbled to Skeeter.

The lead teller poked her head out from the bank's door. "You men shouldn't be standing here."

"Why not?" Jack asked.

"Because it doesn't look good."

"Well, toodooledo on you." He frowned. "Now how does this look?" he asked, making a face. She slammed the door in disgust. "Guess she don't know how to take a joke."

Half the shops along Main Street were shut down with "Back in Two Hours" signs hung in the windows. Even the bank was barely running with just two tellers.

"What kind of work you figure he's got for us?" Skeeter asked.

Jack shrugged impatiently. "You need to earn 'nough to feed yourself. I'll go broke if I have to stuff your face." He saw the bank teller looking out at them again.

Skeeter shrugged. "Man's gotta eat every day to live."

"But you like to eat every day all day," Jack said, eyeing a hobo coming toward him that he hadn't seen in town before.

Adam Cole slouched down in the old clothes he'd stolen from the church box. With ashes on his face and an old hat pulled down over his ears, he hoped no one would recognize him as the owner of the sideshow. But he remembered Railroad Jack and spoke directly to him.

"Mr. Jack," Cole began, putting on a deep Southern accent, "boss man said to tell you and the rest of men that needs work that I should give you each 'nother dollar and to tell you to come over to the sidewalk in front of the bank to wait."

"For how long?" Skeeter asked.

Cole shrugged, pleased that no one had recognized him. "Until you're told to move."

The hoboes crowded forward, reaching out their hands, gladly accepting the crisp dollar bills. Sniffing them, pulling them, holding them up to the light to make sure they were real, the hoboes were all suddenly caught up in a dollar daze.

Skeeter held his up to the light and smiled. "Gonna eat good tonight." The other hoboes were already feeling good and carrying on about what they were going to be doing with the money.

Jack watched the new hobo handing out the money and whispered to Skeeter, "Ain't never met a hobo yet who gave away money."

"The boss man probably trusts him."

"No one trusts a hobo. They think we're thieves."

"Most are."

Cole held up his hands. "Gotta go get more money. Lots more to pay you for the work you'll be doin'."

"Should we follow you?" a hobo called out.

"Just stand over in front of the bank. I'll give you another half day's pay if you promise to come back in the morning." The drifters followed him across the street like he was the Pied Piper.

Jack didn't move. "Hoboes just don't go 'round handin' out money to hoboes. And no one pays hoboes in advance."

"This one does. Let's go and get our pay."

"Pay for what?"

"For tomorrow's work," Skeeter exclaimed. "I'm already gettin' kinda tired from all the work I'm a thinkin' I'll be doin'."

Jack shook his head. "You ever heard of a hobo gettin' paid in advance to work and then showin' up?"

"First time for everything."

"Not for hoboes. We are hoboes 'cause we hate to work. What say you and me go on back and 'round up our things."

"Why for?"

"Why for I say so—that's why for. I just got me a feelin' that John Q. Law is gonna come roust us for hangin' 'round in public."

"You wanna pass up the money tree man?"

"Sometimes you got to know when to fold your cards and leave the game." Jack began walking back toward the railroad tracks. "You comin'?" he asked Skeeter.

Skeeter hesitated. The other hoboes were already waiting on the sidewalk in front of the bank. "I could sure use that money," he grumbled, then he started after Jack.

Cole's heart was beating fast. He gripped tightly the handle of the bank's door before pulling it open. The pistol under his ratty old coat hung heavy. What he was about to do would change his life forever.

I can still turn back. Count my losses and go back to the show.

But if he did that, he'd never get to Mexico. Or be the king of the road or the toast of the country. *I'll be workin', payin' off the debt forever. With the bank's money I can pay off Stein and leave here a free man.*

In his mind he knew that if he found the courage to rob the bank, he'd just up and leave. Paying the debt to Stein with cash after the bank was robbed would be asking to have a noose put around his neck.

Keeping his show *and* keeping the bank's money had been in the back of his mind all along. All he needed was courage.

"Hey, buddy, what you waitin' for?" one of the drifters asked him.

"Just thinkin' 'bout somethin' " Cole said as he pushed open the door.

No customers were in the bank—just two tellers who were wishing they were at the show.

"What do you want?" the older teller asked rudely, sniffing the air, clearly displeased by the presence of a hobo in the bank.

"Shaddup," Cole growled, pulling out his pistol. The ladies gasped. "You're gonna hang out the 'Closed' sign and pull the shades down, understand?"

The tellers didn't move; they stood still, wishing that the no-account hobo would just disappear.

"Either you do as I say or I'll drop you where you stand. I don't care beans 'bout you. I just want the money." The women didn't move. "You both might be plug ugly, but my buddies outside are just waitin' for me to give the word." The ladies looked at the group of dirty, scruffy no-goods on the sidewalk out front. "Just do as I say and you won't get hurt."

Finally the older teller moved around the counter and walked toward the door. After she hung the sign, Cole directed the other teller to pull the shades down.

"Now, pony up. Give me your money. All of it. Put it in here," Cole ordered, pulling an old pillowcase out of his pocket.

With each banded stack of bills that they dropped in, Cole knew that Mexico was getting closer. In his mind he could hear the *mariachi* music, see the pretty senoritas, and smell the fried goat and chicken hanging over big fires.

After tying up the tellers, he said to them, "Ain't right that you rich folk have all the money and us hoboes don't have nothin'. This is just evening the score in my mind."

He lifted two of the stacks of bills from the pillowcase and walked out the front door where the hoboes were gathered. "Here, you men divide this up between yourselves. I'll be back with more in a few minutes."

The hoboes were beside themselves, pulling and pushing to get the bills. "And you hold this," Cole said to the nearest hobo, handing him the pistol.

Taking the alleys, Cole was back in his wagon, cleaned up, changed back into his own clothes, and up on the stage in time to close the show. Giving the sheriff, Givens, and Maurice each a final handshake, Adam Cole waved his arms to end the last show in Mansfield.

24

Following the Tracks

❖

Terry decided to follow the train tracks, wondering where he'd go first. Cicadas and bullfrogs sang loudly. Birds cawed overhead. Terry jumped over a tiny brook and remembered the time he'd lain on his back, thinking he was dying with a green apple bellyache. The smell of honeysuckle rode in on the breeze, lifting his spirits.

"Maybe I ought to catch a train and go to China. Yes sir, just ride it until I get there and then catch me a train and ride to Egypt," he said. He had no idea about oceans or the more basic elements of traveling. All he knew was that he had left home and was embarking on the biggest adventure of his life.

Jumping a train was something the kids in town talked about. It sounded easy enough, but when the first train came racing by Terry stood back in awe, wondering how anybody could get up the nerve to run and grab on. "Guess I'll just wait for a slow-moving one," he mumbled, following the tracks toward town.

After watching a fox stalk a meadow mouse and picking a handful of wild red raspberries, he was tired. He needed some energy, so he stopped and carefully lifted the sugar bowl out of the pillowcase. It was already half empty since he'd stopped a dozen times in the past hour to taste the white sweetness.

"Just one more little lick," he whispered, his eyes wide, as the sun sparkled off the crystal white granules. One lick led to two, then three, and soon he had the sugar bowl tipped high above his head.

"That's my favorite lunch," he smiled, burping loudly to the world.

"No one can tell me to 'cuse myself anymore," he said as he burped again. "I'm a free man!" he shouted.

Railroad Jack sat on a ledge watching Terry. He leaned over to Skeeter and whispered, "I told that fool boy not to run away."

"Think you ought to maybe take him back home?" Skeeter asked.

"Nope. He'll go home soon. You can count on that. Come on, let's go."

Terry caught their movement from the corner of his eye. "That's Railroad Jack," he whispered, putting the empty sugar bowl carefully back into his pillow sack.

"Hey, wait up!" he called out. "I runned away and came lookin' for you. Knew I'd find you if I sniffed 'round."

Jack fumed at the kid's pun and did not stop walking or turn around.

Skeeter looked back. "Looks like he's comin'."

"Don't say a word. Just keep walkin'."

Terry caught up with them in a minute. "Hey, Mr. Jack, where we goin'?"

"'We'?" Jack echoed.

"Yeah, you and me and this man here," Terry said, nodding toward Skeeter.

"My name's Skeeter," the old man said, reaching out his hand toward Terry, who shook it quickly.

"Where we goin' then?" Terry asked.

"There's a difference between 'we' and 'you.' We—meanin' Skeeter and me—are goin' to wherever our feet take us. You—meanin' the redheaded squirrel-brain standin' next to me—are goin' home 'cause I don't need any more travelin' companions."

"Can't go back. My home's on the road with you."

"No, it isn't."

"Yes, it is," Terry said, mustering up the most confident tone he could. "I runned away. Left a note sayin' how I felt. I can't never go back home now."

Jack stopped and put his sack down. "Okay then, you got that lucky nickel you spoke about?"

"Right here," Terry beamed, holding it up. "Pa said it would take me to faraway places, so that's where I'm goin'."

"If you brought your nickel then I guess you're serious," Jack said. He wanted to take the boy by the hand and lead him home, but he knew that unless Terry learned the value of what he was leaving, he would just run away again. "You're really runnin' away?" he asked.

"I am. I'm ready to hobo my way to China."

"You ain't been taught yet."

"Taught what?"

"Taught how to be a hobo."

"Where do I learn?"

"It'll cost you all the money you got to learn the ten secrets of how to be a hobo. You ready to learn?"

"But I only gots a nickel." Terry squeezed it tightly in his palm.

"That's 'nough to be taught the hows and whys and ways of hoboin'. Now, I asked if you're ready to learn the ten secret fine arts and ways of bein' a professional hobo."

Terry looked at his special nickel. It was his only link to his father. "How 'bout I owe you a nickel?"

"How 'bout you go drink from a pig's trough."

"But I don't want to lose my nickel."

"Then you don't get to learn the secrets, which means you can't come with us."

"Okay, but these ten secret things better be worth it." Terry figured he'd work a way to not give over the nickel, but Jack snatched it from his hand.

"Hey, that's mine!"

"Mine now. And that's lesson one. Say and do whatever you have to do to survive."

Terry frowned, wondering if the man was serious about keeping his nickel. "What's lesson two?"

"Lessons two through nine are say and do whatever you have to do to survive."

"But that was lesson one," Terry protested.

"The one and only way of life for hoboes is survivin'. Ain't that right, Skeeter?" Skeeter nodded. Jack looked at Terry. "You still want to come along?"

"I'm gonna follow you 'till I get my nickel back."

"Then you run and get us some hobo walkin' sticks 'bout five feet long and for free I'll show you how hoboes walk."

Skeeter leaned over and whispered to Jack as Terry ran off, "What you want to take his lucky nickel for? Ain't nothin' to teach 'bout hoboin' 'cept keep away from marryin' women, avoid the police, and never take full-time work."

Jack shook his head. "This ain't no life for a boy with a good family. Heck, ain't no life for anyone at all 'cept for ol' fools like us. If it costs him his nickel to learn that, it'll be the best money he ever spent."

"You gonna give him his nickel back then?"

Jack shrugged. "By dark he'll want to be home in his bed. We'll let him hang around long enough to send him on his way, then maybe I'll give him his nickel back."

"What we gonna do?"

"We're gonna hitch a ride on the circus wagons and follow them wherever they're goin'."

"They ain't goin' by train from here?"

"I hear some are and some are splittin' off to work the smaller towns."

Terry came running back with three sticks and began his hobo walking lessons. Jack took the stick and did a kind of funny, bent-over wiggle-walk. "Just keep puttin' one foot in front of you, that's the only way you know you'll get someplace for free."

"Gee, Mr. Jack, this is gonna be fun." Terry smiled, then he began whistling "Yankee Doodle."

"Stop that," Jack commanded.

"But I like to whistle."

"And I *don't* like whistling."

"And I paid my money and now I'm a hobo, so I can whistle if I want to," Terry said, starting back into the chorus.

After the thirteenth version of "Yankee Doodle," Jack was fit to be tied. "What's it gonna take to get you to shut up that whistle?"

"Just give me my nickel back."

"Nope. Can't do that," Jack said, walking as far ahead of the kid as he could.

Skeeter tapped Terry on the shoulder. "Don't you know a different song?"

"I'll just keep whistling until he gives my nickel back."

"Then boy, you're gonna be whistling 'till my hair grows back or your lips fall off."

25

Reward

❖

The town was in an uproar over the hobo bank robbery. The sheriff didn't have to look further than the saloon to find a group of cash-carrying hoboes, buying drinks like they'd just struck it rich.

When he searched the ratty group and found the man carrying the pistol, the sheriff was certain that he had solved the crime, except he could not find the rest of the money. Of course the hoboes denied everything and told him about a man who had been handing out money.

"You boys been drinkin' too much," the sheriff laughed as he locked them up.

"We be tellin' the truth. A man was payin' us for workin' in advance."

"Uh-huh, and my name is Ichabod Crane. No one pays hoboes in advance. Who'd be that stupid? Why don't you boys save me the trouble and tell me where the rest of the money is."

No one knew "nothing about anything." All they could say was that a hobo had given them money outside the bank.

"You boys just spend the night here dryin' out and then I'll ask you again," the sheriff said patiently.

"You can ask Railroad Jack," one of the hoboes pleaded. "He'll tell you what happened."

"And where might I find this Mr. Jack?"

The hobo shrugged. "Heard he was thinkin' 'bout headin' south with another man he hooked up with."

The sheriff didn't pay much heed to the mention of Jack's name until he heard the teller describe the hobo as part of the group of drifters who had surrounded the bank. And there was a smart-mouthed one who called himself Railroad Jack.

"And you think this Jack character had somethin' to do with the robbery?"

"He was hanging around the bank. Even came inside to have me change a dirty ten-dollar bill."

The sheriff then talked with the bank manager, who was distraught. "We lost over twenty thousand dollars, Sheriff. If we don't get that money back, the bank might go under."

A thousand-dollar reward was posted. Sheriff Peterson set out to find out where the character called Railroad Jack might have gone.

When the Springers brought Larry and Sherry home, they found Rev. Youngun sitting on the front steps, his face in his hands. A red ball and a crumpled piece of paper were in his hand.

"He's gone," he whispered.

Sherry began crying for no reason. She just knew that when her father was scared and worried, something really bad had happened.

"Who's gone?" Maurice asked, giving his wife a something's-wrong look.

"Terry. I went over to Reece's to pick him up, but Reece said that Terry had disappeared. So I came back here and found these," Rev. Youngun said, holding up the good-bye notes. "There was a pile of his dirty clothes and these notes. He's gone."

Eulla Mae gasped. They searched the house and barn and looked through the fields, but they didn't find Terry. Maurice rode Larry's horse back to his farm to see if Terry had gone there, but he wasn't there either.

When he got back, Sherry was whimpering. Larry couldn't believe that his squirrelly brother had run off.

"What we gonna do, Pa?" Larry asked.

"We have to go see if he's at any of the neighbors," Rev. Youngun said hopefully.

Maurice looked at Larry and Sherry. "Terry's been talkin' 'bout runnin' away. Where you think he went?"

Larry thought for a moment, then answered, "Maybe he ran off to see the circus."

"Or join the circus." Maurice nodded.

Grasping at any hope, Rev. Youngun called the sheriff, but he was too busy interrogating the crowded cells of hoboes to be of much help. "He's probably just hidin' in the woods," Sheriff Peterson said. "The kid'll be back by morning."

Rev. Youngun, Eulla Mae, and Sherry set out in the wagon to go see if the neighbors had seen Terry. Maurice and Larry rode into town on their horses to ask around, but no one had seen Terry Youngun. It was as if he'd dropped off the face of the earth.

"Think we better get Dangit and try to follow his tracks," Maurice said as they rode back home.

While the sheriff was questioning every bad egg and drifter he could find, Adam Cole quietly packed up his show and waited for darkness. The big circus tent was struck with all the usual fanfare while Cole sat in his wagon. Stein walked in puffing on a briar pipe like a hay fire racing with the wind.

"Here's your take," Stein said, pushing open Cole's wagon door without knocking. He handed Cole enough money to pay his performers, buy feed for his mules and horses, with only a little left over for pocket change.

"I've paid you back all I borrowed and then some," Cole grumbled, wishing he could reach into the pillow sack of cash hidden under the table and stuff the bills into the circus owner's mouth.

"You're still payin' off the interest. Once that's done you'll start payin' back the money you borrowed," Stein replied.

"Don't seem right that you can charge me twenty percent a month in interest."

"That's my rate. You didn't have to borrow the money. I warned you."

"Bet you're upset about the robbery," Cole said to change the subject.

Stein chuckled. "You think I'd trust a yokel bank with my money?"

"Then you didn't lose much?" Cole didn't let his disappointment show.

"Not enough to hurt. But the town won't charge me no fee now for settin' up so I'll make out on the deal," Stein said as he slammed the door behind him.

Cole knew now that he would never repay the man. *I'm takin' that money and goin' to Mexico.*

On the Road

❖

As much as he hated to admit it, Jack kind of liked having Skeeter and the boy around, even if Terry was an obnoxious whistler who kept asking him why he never took baths. The fact was that Jack saw that Terry was a curious kid. He asked questions about everything. In a way he reminded Jack of himself back in a time when his life was still innocent. Before he himself had run away and taken on his own heavy load of guilt.

As they walked further and further away from his home, Terry wondered if anybody cared that he was already halfway to China. "Sure wish we was ridin' in a car," he mumbled.

"Can't drive and don't want to," Jack said curtly.

"Beats walkin'."

"The day you get me in a car is the day I'll give your lucky nickel back," Jack declared.

"If I was grown up I'd wup the tar outta you." Terry glared.

Jack laughed. "Son, boys can't wait to grow into men, but the truth is we never grow up. We just go on actin' like boys in old bodies."

Terry didn't understand what Jack was talking about, but he just nodded as if he understood every word. All he could think of was to whistle some more, which nearly drove Jack up a tree. As dusk began swallowing the afternoon, the two of them came to a truce of sorts. Terry agreed to stop whistling if Jack would agree to give his nickel back.

"One nickel's the same as another. What's so special 'bout that one?"

"Got my own reasons, and you gypped me on that hobo lesson anyway."

"Best lesson you'll ever learn. I probably saved you from a life of misery."

"You sure talk like you know it all."

Jack winked at Skeeter. "Mr. Redhead, I've done everything and been just about everywhere. There ain't nothin' you can ask that I probably haven't learned somethin' 'bout the hard way."

"How come *you're* so quiet?" Terry asked Skeeter.

"Me, why, I ain't much for talkin' 'bout myself like Mr. Jack is."

"You got some free lessons you want to learn me?"

"Just do your washin' downstream from folks you're travelin' with and do your drinkin' upstream. Remember that, and you won't get nobody mad at you," Skeeter said.

Terry grinned. "Guess Mr. Jack ain't never learned the washin' lesson. He kinda stinks."

Jack glared. "Stinks? I'm carryin' road dust from a thousand places. Protects me from gettin' cold."

"Your nose must be broken if you can't smell yourself. My pa would finally let his spankin' hand go to work if I came home stinkin' like a two-legged outhouse."

"You runned away," Jack teased, "so don't be worryin' what your pa would be thinkin'."

"Just get used to his hobo perfume," Skeeter cautioned.

Terry scrunched up his face, looking at the hoboes through one half closed eye, ready to zing back. "Perfume? That'd be like gettin' used to a tree full of road apples."

Jack gave Skeeter a look. "Life's kinda short and full of ticks and skeeters, so don't waste time just yappin' unless you're goin' to be a judge or a preacher."

"My pa's a preacher."

"That figures. Preacher's kids are always the worst," Jack said. "Your daddy should've scrubbed you down with lye soap and gotten the bad outta you."

Terry kicked the ground. "I ain't bad. I'm just hungry."

"Now you want me to rustle up beans. Skeeter," Jack said, shaking his head, "what we gonna do with this kid?"

"All I knows is, I'm hungry too," Skeeter said.

"So am I," Terry said again, feeling like one of the hobo guys now.

"That's all I need," Jack groaned, "two maggots wantin' to eat up all my grub money."

"You got any food in that sack of yours?" Skeeter asked Terry.

"Just a piece of candy."

"Anythin' else?" Skeeter asked. His stomach growled. The ham and eggs breakfast Jack had bought hadn't been enough.

Terry took out the sugar bowl. "Had me a full bowl of sugar, but I already ate it."

Jack cocked his head. "You mean to tell me you ate a whole bowl of sugar on your way here from your house?" He was still hungry too.

Terry nodded with a serious look. "Walkin' always makes me powerful hungry."

"Well," Jack began, "if that's the case then you might as well go back home. We ain't but five miles from your place and you already ate a quarter's worth of sugar. You're too expensive to feed."

"Sorry," Terry said, looking down.

"Wish you'd brought a pie," Skeeter sighed. "A strawberry or apple pie."

"Or a blueberry pie," added Jack. His stomach growled again.

"Or maybe a blackbird pie." Skeeter grinned.

"You eat pies made from birds?" Terry asked, not believing his ears.

"Any kind of pie's all right by me, but fruit pie's best." Jack sighed.

"I ain't seen the spoon bottom of a fruit pie pan for 'bout two years," Skeeter said. "Not since that church down in Ark-can-saw invited me to the church supper."

Jack nodded. "I ain't seen the top or bottom of a home-cooked pie in so long I can't even remember when."

"Eulla Mae makes real good pies," said Terry.

"Who's that?" Jack asked.

"She's the neighbor lady who helps us out."

"Kinda like a stepmama?" Skeeter asked.

"Kinda," Terry said, wondering if Eulla Mae would miss him as much as he already missed her.

They walked along, each dreaming about pie, until Skeeter began to sniff the air. "You smell what I smell?"

Jack sniffed the air like a hound dog. "We ain't dead, is we?"

Skeeter pinched himself. "Nope. But I do swear that I'm smellin' a pie in the air."

Terry spun around in a circle, then stopped, scuffling the ground, sniffing up a load of air. "It's comin' from over there," he said, pointing to the rectory of the Catholic hall.

"Let's go see if maybe they're in the sharin' mood," Jack said, leading the way. "You see, little Red, hoboes get fed when they act all down and hungry."

"I ain't actin'. That part comes natural to me," Skeeter declared.

When they got up to the edge of the bushes, Jack signaled for everyone to squat down. They could see the pie on the kitchen window ledge, fresh-baked hot with wispy steam curls circling in the air. The rectory housekeeper leaned out of the kitchen window to check on the pie.

Skeeter breathed deeply. "That's definitely an apple pie."

Jack pulled Terry to his side. "Okay, Red, here's your chance to earn your hobo stripes."

"My what?"

"That's just hobo army talk. I want you to march right up there and get us that pie."

"You mean steal it?"

"Borrow it. There's a difference."

"What's the difference? You want me to steal the pie so we can eat it.'

"No, I want you to bring me the pie so we can borrow the pie pan. Then, when we're finished cleanin' the pan, you can take it back."

Terry could smell the sweet cinnamon sprinkled on the baked apples in the pie. His stomach groaned. "Do I get first bites?"

"Boy," Skeeter said, "Lord helps those who help theyselves. Go get the pie, Red, and help yourself to your fill."

Terry looked at the two men. "Don't remember my pa preachin' 'bout the goodness of stealin'."

"I told you," Jack repeated, "this ain't stealin', it's borrowin' so the church can help feed the poor."

"It's thievin'," Terry argued. "I don't mind doin' it, but I don't like you paintin' it for somethin' it ain't."

The two men looked at him as a robin strutted by with its head cocked, not paying them a bit of attention.

"I'm gonna go do somethin' wrong and I know it. You two want to hide behind words and pretend like you don't know what you're doin'." Terry marched off toward the pie.

As he walked off Jack shook his head. "He'll never make a good hobo."

"Why not?" Skeeter asked.

"'Cause he's got a conscience."

Terry made his way through the formal flower gardens, past the wrought iron benches, around the birdbaths and stone markers until he was near enough to scout out the area and decide what to do. The closer Terry got to the window the more frightened he got. His eyes were on the ground, and suddenly he ran head-on into a marble statue of Mother Mary, with one eye weathered off.

"Holy smokes," he whispered, backing up and knocking over a pedestaled sundial.

Replacing it quickly, he quick-stepped along a row of statues then froze in place next to a St. Christopher statue as a large, leaded-paned door opened onto the rectory balcony. A priest came out and stretched, looking out over the gardens. Terry tried to look like one of the statues, freezing with his arms in the air.

I know he's gonna see me, Terry worried, his knees wanting to knock and shake.

Terry held his pose for another minute until the priest walked back inside.

Gulping for air and courage, he snuck up under the window and reached up and touched the edge of the pie pan.

"Ouch." It was hot. Too hot to carry.

There were corn husks in a pile by the back door. *Someone's been sittin' out here shuckin' corn. Gotta be quick.* He could smell corn bread hot from the oven and coffee brewing in a tin kettle.

Taking out his two pairs of socks from his sack, Terry put them over his hands and reached up for the pan. With a little jiggling, he managed to lift it off the ledge. The sweet cinnamon sauce oozed from the slits in the top of the pie.

"They'd want us to have it—us being so hungry and all," he whispered, trying to ease his conscience.

Then he looked at his two partners in crime. If he got caught, they'd run.

He touched the top of the pie, but it was still steaming warm. *I deserve first piece*, he thought. He stuck his finger through the brown crust.

"Hey, Red, bring that pie back here," Jack hissed.

"Hold on," Terry said, licking the sauce off his finger. *That's good. Can't put it back now,* he thought, looking at the finger hole in the middle of the crust. The deed had been done. He looked at the pie and brought it up to his nose. *Wish I had me a spoon.* He tried sticking his tongue into the pie and burned it. "Ouch!"

"Bring that pie here," Jack ordered.

Terry didn't move. "Those two tramps will eat it all," he mumbled, letting it cool for a moment. Then he stuck his hand back into the pie and lifted up a dripping piece.

Skeeter couldn't believe it. "That kid's eatin' our pie."

"That little tramp," Jack growled, forgetting that it wasn't really his pie to begin with.

"Kid's eatin' like a rat in the pantry," Skeeter said. Then he saw the housekeeper looking out from the window, searching for her pie. "We gots trouble."

"No," Jack said, "*he* gots trouble."

"What are we gonna do?"

"*We* is gonna sit here to see how *he* gets out of it. Good time to see what kind of tramp he really is."

Terry was sucking and slurping and gobbling up the pie as fast as he could. He was so busy eating that he didn't notice the housekeeper standing on the porch steps, wiping her hands on her apron.

"And what are ye doin'?" she asked in a thick Irish brogue.

"Me?" Terry asked innocently.

"Yes, you with the pie all over your mouth. That's the pie for the priest's supper."

The woman was big, with the full, large frame of a woman raised on hard work. She slowly tapped a big wooden spoon against her thigh, waiting for Terry to answer. He figured she was gonna swat him if he didn't come up with a whopper of an excuse, so he concentrated as hard as he could.

Skeeter figured Terry was going to get whupped too. "Boy better talk fast."

"Better run fast if you ask me or he's dead meat," Jack said, wondering what Terry would do.

Terry put the pie down and wiped his mouth on his sleeve. "I couldn't help myself. I know I sinned, but I was so hungry that I'd have eaten the Ten Commandants to get to that pie."

The housekeeper immediately softened, remembering all the street urchins she had seen in New York when she had landed at Ellis Island on her way from Ireland. The homeless orphans. The little girls selling day-old flowers. The ones who had indentured themselves to the ragpickers to survive.

"My poor boy. Where are your parents?"

"My ma died of the fever. And I been workin' pickin' carrots for longer than I can remember."

"Pickin' carrots?"

"Yup, have a brother and sister to feed. Now they're bein' raised by a minister, and I left to make my fortune to bring back money and help them out."

"Make your fortune? But you're nothin' but a little boy."

"It's an almighty hard life I've been livin'."

"Well, you come inside and I'll make you a sack of food."

"That'd be right nice." Terry nodded, then turned and gave the hoboes a nose willy.

Jack shook his head. "If I hadn't seen this with my own eyes I'd have sworn you just conjured it up," he said to Skeeter.

Terry carried the sack lunch and what was left of the pie back to the bushes. Jack was fit to be tied. Skeeter dug right into the sack of food, but Jack had wanted that pie and now there were only some pieces of crust left.

"You ate the whole durned thing," Jack said.

"Lord helps those who help themselves." Terry shrugged, wiping his face with his sleeve.

Jack looked down at the remains of the pie. "You didn't leave enough to fill up a hummingbird."

"If you don't want it I'll eat it," Terry said, licking his lips.

"Jack," Skeeter said, munching on the food in the sack, "just dig in to some of this."

Jack fluttered his lips in deep frustration. "Kid, just don't start whistlin'," he warned, picking up a little hunk of the gooey crust that Terry had left him.

Skeeter patted Terry on the head. "Kid, you're gonna make a good tramp yet."

"Not on my watch," Jack said. He held Terry by the shoulders. "Red I want you to go back home. I want you to go home and hug your papa and work things out."

"I can't."

"You can."

"But I runned away."

"And you can run back home." Jack stooped down and looked Terry in the eyes. "Kid, believe me, livin' on the road ain't no fun. It ain't no life at all."

"But you like it."

"Maybe I just make out like I like it. If I had a home to go back to, I'd be there now and never leave. But I can't. I made my bed, and I got to sleep with the nightmares I told you 'bout."

"'Bout not sayin' good-bye."

"About not sayin' that and a whole lot of other things." Jack stood up. "Now scoot. Go on. I don't ever want to see your face again."

"But I want to come with you."

"Go home."

"I can't."

"You will."

"I ain't goin without my lucky nickel."

"I'll mail it to you," Jack said, walking off.

Terry grabbed on to his pant leg. "Give me my nickel."

"Leave me alone, kid, and go home."

With that, Jack grabbed Skeeter's arm and began walking away, ignoring Terry's cries. "You can't just leave him like that," Skeeter said.

"I can and I did. Goin' home is best for that kid."

"At least give him his nickel back."

"Now don't look back. It's gettin' candle lightin' dark, so he'll get scared and run back home."

Terry watched them go, wondering what he should do.

27

Off to Mexico

❖

As darkness fell, Cole hooked his car up and instructed Roger to form up the wagons and head south. All he had to do was cross the border into Mexico before Stein or the law caught up to him. Then he would be able to keep his sideshow *and* the bank money.

"Now?" Roger questioned. "But the circus is headin' off to Memphis in the mornin'."

"We've got some business to do down south. Here's a bonus for helpin' me," Cole said, handing Roger two hundred dollars.

Roger whistled. "Why you handin' me money just like that?"

"'Cause if you help get me where I'm goin', I'll rip up the note you signed and free you from your debt."

"Why you bein' good to me like that all of a sudden?"

"Let's just say my luck's changed. Now let's get goin'."

"Where south are we goin'?"

"Just keep drivin' until they don't speak English anymore."

"Louisiana?" Roger exclaimed, remembering the funny way that the Cajun folk talked around Baton Rouge.

"No, Mexico. Get me to the border, and I'll give you another two hundred bucks. But don't tell anyone in the show where we're goin', and lock Jo-Jo up in the back of my wagon." Jo-Jo was the only one in the sideshow who spoke Spanish, and Cole didn't want him to run away.

Roger took Jo-Jo from his sleeping wagon and locked him in the back of Cole's. "Just doin' my job," he said to the hairy boy.

Cole finished writing a note to Stein, saying that he was going to do a quick show in St. Louis and would rejoin the circus in Memphis. "By the time they get to Memphis, I'll be long gone to Mexico," Cole chuckled as he left the note under Stein's door.

They rode south out of Mansfield, six sideshow wagons creaking along the potholed road, towing Cole's precious car behind them. Although no one knew it but Cole and Roger, they were off to Mexico where Cole was intent on being the sideshow king.

He talked to Roger through the window from inside the wagon.

"Keep your eye out for any riders comin' up behind us."

"You expectin' anyone, boss?"

"Nope, but we can't be too careful. And make sure you don't take no big bumps. Don't want nothin' to hurt my car you're pullin'."

Jo-Jo stared out from the small sleeping quarters in the back of Cole's wagon where he'd been locked up. He missed the Gomez family.

The only thing he had to occupy himself was a pile of paper scraps and a pencil, so Jo-Jo drew strange little pictures of his memories of Mexico, dreaming of the day he would go back there.

"Mr. Cole, where are we going?" he asked.

"To Mexico. Like I told you."

"Is there somethin' you ain't tellin' me, boss?" Roger asked from the front of the wagon.

"Roger, I'm tired of bein' indentured for a gamblin' debt I've paid back five times over."

"You paid off Mr. Stein?"

"I will soon."

"Guess you heard 'bout that bank robbery, didn't you?" Roger asked.

"Some lucky hobo pulled a good one," Cole said.

"He's a rich hobo now. So where are we goin'?"

"Mexico. I'm takin' the show to Mexico where I'm gonna live out my days."

"Where to in Mexico you want me to take you?" Roger asked.

"Just to the border. I can hire someone to take me from there."

Roger was silent for a moment. "And what if I want to come with you?"

"Then I'll double your wages and make you manager of the show."

Roger swelled with pride, not knowing that Cole was leading him on. All Cole wanted to do was get across the border, beyond the reach of the law, and he was willing to do or say anything to get there.

"Just don't let Jo-Jo get away," Cole added.

"What's he done? Why you got him locked in the back of your wagon?" Roger stifled a wheezing cough.

"'Cause he's the only one who knows their language down there."

Jo-Jo had heard it all. Mexico. He was really going home.

No one with Cole's show noticed the two hoboes grab on to the back of the fourth wagon in the line. Sideshows and circuses always had drifters traveling along, so it was easy for Railroad Jack and Skeeter to blend in and hitch as far as they wanted to go. Jack made himself comfortable on the sacks of feed and supplies that Cole's show was carrying. He looked at Skeeter and smiled.

"See, I told you that pie-stealin' kid would go home when I told him to."

Skeeter shook his head. "I still can't believe he ate up all that pie by hisself. But he sure done good gettin' that sack of food."

"I'll starve in silence before I'll eat with 'Yankee Doodle' whistlin' off-key in my ears."

"Thought I was gonna go crazy, him whistlin' that song over and over," Skeeter agreed.

"But I didn't give him his nickel. That boy's goin' home havin' learned hisself a valuable lesson in life."

"You really think he went back?"

"I'll bet his lucky nickel that he's probably home now eatin' a hot supper, huggin' up on his folks, glad he's home."

"I don't know," Skeeter replied. "He looked like a pretty crafty kid."

"He'll do what I told him." Jack looked wistfully toward the stars. "Home's where we all wish we could be."

"That's the real hobo's lonely secret, ain't it, Jack?"

Neither of them saw a redheaded boy with a pillow sack over his arm racing out to climb onto the back of the car being towed behind the last wagon.

"I'm gonna get my nickel back if it's the last thing I do," Terry muttered.

He unsnapped the Oldsmobile's cover and lay on the seat, feeling tired. He looked up at the stars. The sky was massing for rain, but the wind was pulling it south. The horses' hooves from the sideshow wagon train were like night music clopping along. Soon Terry fell asleep to the slow, easy rocking of the road, hoping that his father was sorry he was gone.

There was no turning back now.

28

Tracking

❖

Terry had still not returned by the time Maurice and Larry got back to the Younguns' house. Rev. Youngun was upset, blaming himself for Terry's running away. Rubbing his forehead with one hand, he said, "I should have paid more attention to him. I should have."

"Ain't your fault," Maurice said.

Sherry sat in the corner, whimpering for Terry.

Rev. Youngun looked up. "We have to find him, Maurice."

"Larry and I are gonna keep on lookin'."

"Here, take some money," Rev. Youngun said, opening his wallet. "I'll do anything, pay anything, to get my boy back."

"Don't need your money," Maurice said. "Just your prayers." He looked at Larry. "Bring along two blankets rolled up and some food we can put in the saddlebags. And feed Dangit, 'cause we're gonna be needin' him."

"You bringin' Sausage?" Sherry asked.

"Nope, that fat ol' dog wouldn't make it a quarter mile 'fore he had hisself a heart 'tack," Maurice answered.

Maurice and Larry set out on their horses with Dangit sniffing Terry's tracks. They stopped to check out every weather-beaten house and clapboard shack along the path. They poked around the new squatters' huts with what looked like wax paper windows. There was even a fishing camp with a lean-to of sorts. Larry untied the slimy knot over the door, but only a weasel scurried out.

"Nothin' here, Mr. Springer," Larry said.

"Let's keep lookin'."

They followed the tracks and Terry's scent to the train rails and then through the woods. Everyone they came upon tried to be helpful. An old sunburned farmer wearing a sweat-stained bandanna thought he'd seen a bunch of kids smoking cigarettes in a hollow, but it turned out to be nothing but some farm kids having a get-together.

They rode on, following Dangit past a hobo camp and onto the road south. The further they got from Rev. Youngun's house the more desperate Maurice felt. *That kid's gone further than I thought he would. Hope we find him hidin' out somewhere soon.*

Dangit raced up to the Catholic rectory, howling like he had found Terry. "Think Terry's in there?" Larry wondered.

"You just be hopin' that dog don't go pullin' at no priest's pants."

"Won't happen unless he misuses Dangit's name."

The housekeeper told them about a redheaded boy who ate her pie—and touched her heart. "Said his mother had died and he'd been workin' for years picking carrots. Those were his words."

Maurice wanted to grin but suppressed it. "And do you know which way the boy went?"

"I packed him a sack of food and sent him on his way with God's blessings."

She pointed the direction Terry had gone, and Dangit went racing toward the woods. Maurice and Larry waved good-bye, before the woman could tell them about the good-for-nothing hoboes she had seen following the boy.

"Slow down, Dangit!" Larry shouted.

They found the remains of the sack of food. From the footprints, Maurice deduced that Terry wasn't alone.

"Think he's been kidnapped?" Larry wondered.

"Nope. Looks like Terry's taken up with a couple of kids."

Larry looked around. "He talked about running away and joining the circus."

"Circus ain't left town yet, and his tracks are leading south," Maurice said, getting back up onto his horse. "Let's keep following them."

Along the way they asked everyone they met if they'd seen a redheaded boy traveling alone or with a couple of other kids. No one could remember seeing Terry. Finally, they came upon a dull-looking hobo camping by the road.

"You seen a redheaded boy comin' this way?" Maurice asked.

"Maybe," the tramp shrugged. The lines on his prematurely aged face made it hard to read what he was thinking.

"Might be travelin' with a couple of kids," Larry added, crinkling his nose as he caught a strong whiff of the man's odor.

"Hard to 'member things," the tramp shrugged, turning away as if the conversation were over. He picked at the few teeth he had left with his finger.

"Think 'bout this," Maurice said, holding up a dime.

The tramp took it from his hand and grinned, showing his awful, greenish teeth. "Saw a kid and two joes bumming together."

Maurice's heart jumped. "You did?"

"Yup," the tramp said, and described Terry so perfectly that Maurice knew the tramp was telling the truth.

"You got any idea where they might be headed?"

"Just thataway," the tramp said, pointing down the road.

"Walkin'?"

"Nope." The tramp ran his tongue across his lower lip.

Maurice waited for an answer, but the tramp held out his hand for more money. "Here's another dime," Maurice said impatiently. "Now, how were they travelin'?"

The tramp bit on the dime to make sure it was real. He held it up to the light, looking through his narrow, slit eyes at the coin, then put it into his pocket. "By wagon. Saw 'em with my own two eyeballs sneak a hitch ride on one of the sideshow wagons."

Maurice was anxious to get going. "Anything else?"

"Maybe, but you gotta give me some more money, dangit."

Dangit grabbed at the man's tattered pant leg.

"No, Dangit!" Larry shouted, reaching down to pull the dog away.

"What's wrong with that dog?" the hobo huffed, kicking at the dog once Larry had him in his arms.

"He just don't like anyone misusing his name."

"That dog's crazy," the hobo grumbled.

"Thanks for your help," Maurice nodded.

Dangit sniffed about a hundred yards, and then Terry's trail ended where the wagon wheels had left a deep groove in the road. A sideshow flyer lay crumpled by the wayside. Larry dismounted and picked it up.

"Guess he made good on his threat," Maurice said sadly, hoping the boy was all right.

"He's hip-deep in a world of trouble," Larry said.

"Your daddy just wants him back. Believe me. That's a fact."

They called Rev. Youngun from the nearest working phone at a small store in town and gave him the news.

"Keep following him, Maurice, please," Rev. Youngun said.

"We're doing our best."

"You have to bring back Terry before something bad happens to him," Rev. Youngun whispered, hanging up the phone and looking into the shadows.

Early evening had come and gone. Maurice and Larry rode along the twisting road until it was too dark to see. With no coffee to keep his eyelids up, Maurice called it a night near a fresh-tilled field bordering a small creek. They bought a skinned jackrabbit from a hardscrabble-looking farm boy, along with two potatoes, and spit-roasted their dinner, both trying to make conversation that they didn't feel like making. As the rabbit juices spittled up the fire, Maurice looked into the flames, seeing all the worst possible outcomes for Terry.

Back in Mansfield, Rev. Youngun lit a candle in the front window and sat up, watching the driveway, wishing that a small, redheaded boy would come walking back home. Sherry slept on his lap, but Rev. Youngun felt alone. Terribly alone.

29

Posse

❖

Sheriff Peterson looked at the band of volunteers who had gathered in his office—farmers, merchants, and a few local farmhands. Some were carrying deer rifles; others clutched antique pistols left over from the Civil War.

"You men know what's at stake here," he said. The men nodded agreement. "The bank lost twenty thousand dollars. That's the lifeblood of this town. Without that money people won't get paid, stores won't be able to buy goods, and some folks might go hungry."

"Why aren't we ridin' out now to find the hobo crooks?" a young farmer asked, reaching down to pull up his drooping socks.

"No sense tryin' to track in the dark. What I want each of you to do is come back at daylight with a good horse and a sleepin' blanket. We'll start on the trail tomorrow."

"You got any clues?" an older man asked.

"The tellers at the bank are convinced that a hobo named Railroad Jack is connected to this," the sheriff said.

"The genius hobo?"

"The same one."

"You see it that way?"

"All I see is a bank that might go under if we don't find that money. I'm gonna sweat the hoboes I got locked up to see what else they know." Then, as if an afterthought, he held up a picture of Terry Youngun that Maurice had delivered. "You all know Rev. Youngun's kid, Terry."

"What in sam hill did he do now? Rob the bank?" one of the merchants asked.

"No, he's run away and the reverend is mighty upset."

"Boy couldn't have got far," the farmer said. "Probably just hidin' in the woods."

"Maybe, but if you see him or hear anything 'bout him, let me know. His brother says that Terry's been talkin' 'bout runnin' away from home for a couple weeks now."

"Heard there's a bear been tearin' up livestock in the next county over. The boy better be careful out there."

"Gentlemen," the sheriff said, raising his hand for silence, "we've got to catch us some bank robbers in the morning. And hopefully find us a runaway kid, God willin'."

After the posse volunteers left, the sheriff suffered through calls from the mayor, the bank manager, and a dozen merchants who were worried about what would happen to Mansfield if the bank went under. Though his eyes hung heavy with dark circles, Sheriff Peterson was determined not to rest until he found the bank's money; he knew his own job was at stake. If the bank went under, the town would be ruined—and he'd be out of work.

He heard from the housekeeper at the Catholic rectory about a little boy who was on her mind, hoping that someone would find him and take him to an orphanage. Then the housekeeper mentioned that she thought she'd seen two questioable-looking older men following the boy.

"They were probably trying to steal the bag of food that I gave the lad."

"And what did these two men look like?"

Embarrassed, she finally said, "Bums. A white man and a black man."

"You mean hoboes?"

"Yes. And that's why I'm worried about the redheaded lad."

Reverend Youngun called right after that with the same information, saying it had to be Terry. The sheriff sent one of the deputies to follow up on the lead. The deputy found that a group of circus wagons had passed near the rectory heading south toward Arkansas. After questioning the group of carnies and roustabouts who were packing up the circus, the sheriff went to see Mr. Stein to ask him if any wagons had already left.

"I'm missing a sideshow. How did you know?"

"The sideshow's missing?"

"Took off in all the confusion after the robbery. Left me a note saying they were going north to St. Louis to work a quick show."

"St. Louis? You sure?"

Stein showed him the note from Adam Cole. "I've got contacts in St. Louis. I'll be checkin' on him."

Peterson shrugged. "I heard the wagons are heading south."

"South?" Stein exclaimed.

"That's what I heard."

"Cole owes me a bundle of money. There's no place in this country that I won't go to collect it."

With the hoboes and Terry Youngun heading the same direction as the sideshow wagons, Sheriff Peterson took a long-shot guess and figured that the hoboes and Terry might have hitched a ride. He figured Adam Cole was trying to leave the state to escape paying his debts. And hoboes always loved a free ride on a wagon.

Sheriff Peterson took two men and rode after Cole's wagons, taking the southern trail that was shorter but more difficult than the road Cole was on. The sheriff knew a retired deputy who lived on a farm along the south trail where they could stay for the night. "We'll catch up with 'em before they get to the Arkansas fork," he told his men.

They rode through the Ozark night under the white sickle of a moon in the sky, riding fast to catch up with a freak show, two hoboes, and a feisty, runaway kid.

30

Holy Smokes

❖

Terry woke up in the star-fire dark. He was stretched out on the seat of Cole's Oldsmobile. He yawned, licking his lips, wishing he had some candy. "Musta fallen asleep," he whispered, looking around, wondering why nothing sounded like his bedroom. Then he remembered where he was and sat up behind the steering wheel.

"This is just like ol' lady Beedlebottom's," he whispered, turning the wheel back and forth. The wagon pulling the car began to sway and buck.

"What's goin' on?" a voice inside the wagon shouted out. Terry slumped down under the dashboard.

"Car wheel musta turned, Mr. Cole," Roger said.

"You shoulda tied the steering wheel straight."

"I'll do it at the next stop."

Terry realized he was too exposed sitting in the car, and he couldn't figure out how to snap the cover back on, so he carefully climbed forward along the hood of the car and jumped onto the wagon. He decided he could hide under the tarp that was covering some boxes. He clung to the handles of the wagon, wondering where he was going. Wedging himself into the overhang under the wagon's roof, he looked through the window. There he saw Adam Cole counting the biggest pile of money he had ever seen.

"Holy smokes, look at that money." Terry leaned around the edge, trying to get a better view through the window, and accidentally knocked loose a crate of flyers which had been tied under the eaves. The wooden box banged against the wall as a bundle of flyers fell loose.

Terry looked down, then back into the window—and straight into Cole's eyes. Before Terry could react, Cole had flung the door open and dragged him inside.

"What were you doing out there?" Cole raged, cuffing Terry with a bone-jarring swat.

Terry wished he could disappear. The man looked mean—real mean. His face was turning red, and the veins were sticking out in his neck.

"Nothin'. Just peekin', that's all," Terry whispered, wanting to cry.

"Peekin' at this," Cole exclaimed, waving his hand toward the pile of money, his face as red as a fireplug. He looked at the boy's young, unlined face and cuffed him again for no reason.

Terry rubbed his head, fighting back tears. "Why you hittin' on me?"

"How did you get here? What were you lookin' in here for?"

"Just curious, that's all," Terry whimpered, his nerves twisting together like snakes in his stomach.

Cole pulled him by the hair toward the back of the wagon. Toward the room where Jo-Jo was locked away.

"Curiosity killed the cat, my red-haired friend," he laughed wickedly, popping Terry again.

"I didn't mean nothin' by it. Let me go. I won't bother you no more."

"You saw the money, didn't you?" Cole asked, figuring that Terry had heard about the bank robbery.

Terry's throat was so tight that it felt like a stick was wedged in it. *Somethin's wrong here,* he told himself.

"You saw my money. Admit it, boy."

"What money? I didn't see that pile of money you got over there."

"We've got ourselves a jim-dandy of a problem, boy," Cole growled harshly. "You know my secret."

Terry shook his head, hoping for a miracle to happen, for someone to save him, but he had run away and no one knew where he was. No one could rescue him now.

Cole shook him hard. "You heard me. I said, you know my secret, don't ya?"

Terry's pulse was beating so hard that his temples hurt. "Don't know any secrets. I'm deaf as a board."

"You're what?" Cole shouted into Terry's face.

Terry tapped his ears. "What? Can't hear you."

Cole slapped Terry's hands down. "You hear good. Are you a runaway?" he asked, looking at the pillow sack in Terry's hand.

Terry shook his head. "I was, but now I'm tryin' to find a hobo named Railroad Jack who's got my lucky nickel."

"Well, since you saw the money, you're comin' along with me."

"No thanks. I better get back on home," Terry said, turning around.

Cole grabbed him by his shirt and yanked him backward. "You can send your folks a letter from Mexico 'cause this is your lucky day."

Terry's heart sank. "Mexico? I wanna go home."

"Too late, kid. I'm between a rock and a hard place. Can't let you walk outta here with my secret."

Cole scraped the money off the table into the pillow sack he'd used in the robbery, and tossed it under the table.

"Let me go!" Terry demanded. He felt lost and empty. It was the worst feeling he'd ever had.

"Shut up, woodpecker. Now get in there," Cole said, pushing Terry into the small sleeping quarters in the back of his wagon and locking the door. "No one knows about the money except for that kid," he mumbled.

Terry wrapped his arms around his knees and began to cry softly. Sitting in the dark room, he wished he had never run away from home. He wished he was back in his warm bed. Wished he had his lucky nickel.

The dark room smelled funny. Like harsh, stale cigarette smoke and human sweat.

Terry began to pray powerfully hard, wishing he were anywhere else on earth but where he was. He bowed his head, clasping his hands tightly. "Please, God, don't let him take me to Mexico. I just wanna go home."

"Why don't you want to go to Mexico?" asked a voice in the dark.

Terry felt spine-chilling goose bumps double ripple up his back, like something was crawling under his skin from a nightmare. He looked with one eye closed into the pool of moonlight. The silence was so fragile that it wouldn't hold a ghost. Then he saw a werewolf standing next to him. A werewolf. An honest-to-God-that's-the-one-from-the-pictures werewolf.

All Terry could think to do was scream like a banshee.

Jo-Jo panicked, not knowing what to do. He hadn't been this close to a boy outside the show in a long time, and this one was throwing a serious conniption fit, wailing and crying like he was dying, his screams slicing through the night.

"Don't eat me, don't eat me!" Terry pleaded, figuring the werewolf was going to rip out his throat and leave him as cold as a wagon tire.

Jo-Jo backed up against the wall. Terry pulled at the door. "Let me outta here! I'm havin' a heart 'tack!"

"Shuddup!" Cole screamed back. "Or I'll tan your hide."

"There's a werewolf in here," Terry whimpered, remembering the picture on the flyer.

"And he'll bite you if you don't shut your yap," Cole growled.

Jo-Jo tapped Terry on the shoulder. Terry froze. "I won't hurt you. I'm human," Jo-Jo said softly.

Terry turned around slowly with a this-ain't-real look on his face. "You can talk."

Jo-Jo nodded. "I just have hair on my body. That's all."

It took Terry a few minutes to adjust, but slowly the light came on in his mind. He realized that Jo-Jo was really human, not a werewolf. Taking a deep breath, he sat down across from the strange-looking boy. A lightning bug flew in through the window and did a whirling dance, giving the boys time to get their courage up.

"Why don't you shave your face off?" It was the only thing Terry could think to say.

"It would just grow back."

Terry cocked his head for a better look. "Don't it itch?"

Jo-Jo shrugged. "Guess I'm used to it. Does your hair ever itch?"

"Sometimes."

"Sometimes my face does too."

Terry felt itchy, trying to imagine what it would be like to have a face covered with hair. "You ever get fleas on your face?"

"I have to take a lot of baths to keep clean."

Terry looked him up and down. "Is your whole body like that?"

"Got hair everywhere except on my lips."

"Everywhere?"

Jo-Jo nodded.

"You ever growl in your sleep?" Terry asked.

Jo-Jo laughed. "No, do you?"

That broke the ice. "What's your name? Mine's Terry. Terry Youngun."

"I'm Jo-Jo."

"You're really the Werewolf Boy?"

Jo-Jo nodded.

"Did you see all that money out there?"

Jo-Jo nodded again. "It looked like a lot."

"Like all the money in the world. Where'd he get it?"

"I don't know. I just work for him."

Terry asked more questions about life with the sideshow. Jo-Jo answered, telling Terry what he knew. Though some of Terry's questions sounded silly, Jo-Jo enjoyed talking to someone who wasn't trying to harass him.

While they talked, Terry starting writing, "Help!" and his name on scraps of Jo-Jo's paper and tossing them out the window, hoping that someone would come looking for him.

"What are you doing here?" Jo-Jo asked.

"I was running away from home until a hobo took my lucky nickel," Terry answered, dropping another note out the window. Terry told Jo-Jo the story of how his father had won the nickel for him. "That hobo, Mr. Jack, hitched a ride on one of those wagons up ahead. I want my nickel back."

"You followed him for a nickel?"

"It's a special nickel that my pa won me. Means everythin' in the world to me."

"Then why'd you run away from home?"

"'Cause my pa was tryin' to make me work in a carrot farm, and he never had time to play with me."

"But he won you the nickel."

"Yeah, that's right," Terry said, sitting quietly, reflecting on the situation he'd gotten himself into.

Jo-Jo put his hands together and looked down. "My father sold me."

"Sold you? Why?"

"Because of the way I looked."

"But you were his kid."

Jo-Jo fought back a tear. "My father said I had to go. I would have never left home if they hadn't made me leave."

Jo-Jo told Terry about the day he was sold. He repeated his mother's last words—how she'd said that he had an angel star in heaven. "And my angel is going to help me get home," Jo-Jo concluded.

"You think?" Terry asked.

"He's already helping me. I'm going to Mexico."

Terry wasn't convinced. "What do you think your angel looks like?"

Jo-Jo thought for a moment, then said, "I don't care what my angel looks like—even if he looks like me." Thumping his chest, he said, "It's what's in here that counts."

They both sat silently for a moment, then Terry spoke up. "But now you're goin' home, right?"

"I'm going back to Mexico. I'd like to see if my mother has a grave."

"But you don't know where to go," Terry said.

Jo-Jo shrugged. "I will find my way."

"Why don't you come back to my house? My pa will help you."

"The man you ran away from?"

"He's a good pa," Terry said defensively. "He works hard. He'd love you too." Silence hung between them as they confronted their lives. Terry suddenly realized what a good man his father was. *I wanna go home. Tell him how I feel.*

"And what about you?" Jo-Jo asked. "What will you do when we get to Mexico?"

The words crashed down on Terry, and he began to cry. He didn't want to go to faraway places under these circumstances. "I wanna go home," he whimpered. "I wanna see my pa."

The wagons creaked along toward Mexico, clicking off miles, as the cicadas sent their songs out on the sultry night wind. Inside, a redheaded child filled with regrets was heading further away from home. Further from where he wanted to be. From where his father was sitting by the phone, waiting for good news.

31

Dawn

❖

Terry sat up stiff-shouldered, trying to unbend from the cramped night's dreamless sleep, but his back was bent up like a horseshoe. His head still hurt from where Cole had smacked him, but that wasn't much on his mind. His first thought was, *Gotta get outta here. Ain't goin' to Mexico.*

The wagons were stopped. He could smell breakfast cooking somewhere outside. Uncomfortable in the cramped space, he looked for a way out but found none. *I gotta get outta here. I gotta figure a way.*

He looked over at his new hairy-faced friend. Terry's original fear had now been replaced by curiosity, and he examined Jo-Jo's face as close as he could without waking the boy. Then he noticed some of Jo-Jo's sketches on scraps of paper and creased his brow, trying to make heads or tales of them.

"Can't believe I slept all night next to a werewolf," he whispered, knowing that if he told anyone about this they'd think his bolts were loose. Terry wrote another note, "Help—Terry Youngun," on one of the scraps and put it aside to toss out of the wagon when they got rolling again.

That's when he heard the tapping on the outside of the wagon and the voice of Railroad Jack. "Hey, Red, is that you in there?"

Jo-Jo awakened, his eyes blinking. A thick tongue darted out, licking the pink lips which stood out from the hairy face. "What was that?"

Terry smelled something like sour milk. "Jack, is that you?" he whispered.

"Yeah. Skeeter and I are here."

"What're you doin' here?"

"That's a question I should ask you," Jack said. "I heard 'em talkin' 'round the cook fires that there was some redheaded kid locked up with a werewolf. Knew they was talkin' 'bout you. You shouldn't have followed us."

"I'm here now, so get me out," Terry said.

"Hold on, pip-squeak. I found this," Jack said, holding up one of Terry's notes. "I found it beside the wagon. You thinkin' this ignorant thing is gonna get you rescued?"

Terry looked down. "I didn't know what else to do."

"Just a much-of-nothin' idea, you leavin' notes like you're Hansel lookin' for Gretel."

"I just wanna go home, Mr. Jack."

Jack chuckled. "I've been tryin' to tell you that there's no place like home, son."

"I wanna take my nickel and go home."

"Nickel, heck boy, I'd have given you one of my nickels if you'd just done what I said."

"But I want *that* nickel. It's special to me," Terry said softly.

"Red, even if you had all the money in the world, you couldn't buy your way back home. You gotta wanna go home with all your heart and soul."

"I do . . . I do," Terry said.

They were both silent for a moment, then Jack asked, "You in there all alone?"

Terry didn't answer right away.

"Who's in there with you, Red?"

"A friend."

"A hairy friend?" Jack whispered, trying to see through the dark window.

"Jo-Jo's okay."

Jack's eyes went wide. "You been in there with a werewolf all night long and you're still alive?"

"Just here with Jo-Jo. He's a friend of mine."

"Looks kinda like man's best friend if you ask me."

"Don't talk like that 'bout Jo-Jo," Terry said defensively.

Jack didn't say anything for a long moment. "You hear 'bout the

Mansfield bank bein' robbed? There's some serious money missin' there."

"The bank was robbed?"

"Yup. Some of the roadies here say some hoboes took the loot."

"How much?"

"Rumor 'round here is 'bout twenty thousand. Wish I had me some of that."

Terry started to tell Jack about the money Cole had but didn't. Instead, he said, "Get me outta here."

"And if I do, will you go home?"

"I'll run all the way home."

"How come they didn't just throw your tail off? That's what they usually do." Before Terry could answer, he heard Jack move away from the wagon. "Red, I gotta go. I see the boss man comin'. Gotta pretend I'm a roadie. I'll be back."

"Get me out!" Terry said, but Jack was already gone.

"Who was that?" Jo-Jo asked.

Terry told him again about his hobo friends. "They ain't no angels, but they're the only chance we got of gettin' outta here."

"Us?"

"Ain't you gonna come too?"

"I want to go to Mexico."

"Why? Your folks are dead."

Jo-Jo went silent, hurt by the simple truth that Terry spoke. Then he began crying. Terry looked down, then said with all the sincerity he could muster, "You think Cole's gonna let you go once you reach Mexico?"

"That man, Mr. Jack, said there's no place like home. That's what I want—a home," Jo-Jo said softly, wiping away the matted tears from the hair on his cheeks.

Terry wanted to hug him but held back, instead patting him on the head. "So do I. So do I."

Jack blended into the camp scene with the rest of the sideshow roadies, swapping stories and trying to make himself useful. He stayed in the shadows, mixing with the two dozen sideshow workers. Skeeter was already helping the cook rustle up breakfast, helping himself to nibbles here and there, taking pieces of the fried salt pork and dipping them into the gravy and brown-sugar syrup.

"Skeeter, come here," Jack said, waving.

Skeeter took another piece of the crisp pork and swallowed it without chewing. "You wanna bite?"

"Just listen to me," Jack said in frustration. He took his friend by the hand off to the side. "It's Red all right."

"Why they got him locked up?"

"I asked him that but couldn't stick 'round for the answer."

Skeeter looked at the cook and pretended to be working. "You want me to lug out another barrel of pork?" he asked the cook, who shook his head no. Skeeter turned back to Jack. "No one knows where we're headed. Some think to Texas and there's whispers about Mexico."

"Mexico?" Jack frowned. "I ain't goin' down there."

"Food's good," Skeeter said. "Cook's got some fried cornmeal mush, prairie chicken hash, and fried salt pork with syrup ready to serve."

"Forget the food. I wanna free up Red and skedaddle on outta here 'fore we get locked up ourselves."

Behind them, the sideshow performers trooped out for breakfast. "Lord help 'em, will you look at them," Skeeter whispered, not believing his eyes.

32

On the Trail

❖

The Gomez family traveled south toward Arkansas. It was the beginning of a long journey that would take them through Texas to Brownsville then over the border into Mexico. They had saved enough money from their work to go home and build a simple block house.

Mr. Gomez clicked the wagon reins, calling out in Spanish to his mules. His wife kept her head on his shoulder until it bumped off. "That Jo-Jo was so sad. All he wanted to do was speak the language," she said.

"I know." He nodded. "I wish we could have brought him with us." Mr. Gomez had worried that Mr. Stein wouldn't give them their last paycheck if he thought they were leaving, so after getting paid, they'd slipped away toward home.

The three girls in the back were busy playing with their rag dolls with dried apple heads that their father had carved. Between them, on a clean rag, was a cornmeal johnnycake they were sharing.

"I'm going to buy you girls some real dolls when we get back home." Mr. Gomez smiled as they squealed with happiness.

Still, he couldn't forget about Jo-Jo. The lost boy with the haunting eyes behind the hood, asking for nothing except Spanish conversation and friendly smiles. Gomez wished he had stolen Jo-Jo away and brought him along to make his angel star dreams come true.

There would have been no sin in stealing a boy away to set him free, he told himself. *I pray his angel comes to help him.*

❖ ❖ ❖

The sheriff and his two deputies traveled the back road, which wasn't much more than an overgrown path in some places. Determined to reach the Arkansas Pass before Cole's wagons got there, Peterson pushed his men and horses hard, trying to make up for their late start.

They had camped for the night in Elmer Stuart's barn. Stuart, a rheumy-eyed, retired deputy sheriff from Wright County who had bought a small, hardscrabble farm for himself and his wife, sat up with them passing a bottle and telling old stories.

Before they'd ridden off at first light, Stuart came out with a pot of hot, black coffee, some corn dodgers, and some final advice. After pouring each man a cup and setting down the tin plate of small cakes his wife had baked in wet corn husks, Stuart said, "Sheriff, it kept me up all night."

"What?"

"The robbery. I've always believed that there's some inner voice you listen to while others are sayin' the obvious."

"What do you mean?"

"What I mean is if hoboes took the money, then it's long gone. You're just whistlin' Dixie. Can't imagine a hobo with a sack of loot hangin' on with circus wagons filled with thievin' carnies who'd clean their mother's clocks."

"What are you sayin', Elmer?" the sheriff asked.

Knocking the dirt off his boots, the former deputy coughed, then said, "I'm sayin' that if things don't look right, then you got to think 'bout lookin' somewhere else."

"Like where?"

"Like why them wagons are heading south instead of north toward St. Louis."

Peterson shook his head. "He's just trying to dodge a debt, that's all."

Elmer wasn't convinced. "Start back at the bank. Think about what happened. Seems that you findin' a group of drunk hoboes standin' at the bar, one of them with a gun, sounds more like you was supposed to find 'em."

"Maybe, maybe not. But chasin' down those circus wagons is the only lead I got. If I don't follow through with it and the money don't never show up, then I'll be blamed for the bank failin'. I gotta try, Elmer. And I gotta try findin' that lost kid."

"Then think it through while you're ridin'. I've always found in the lawman business that if somethin' is too pat you should start lookin' for who stacked the deck."

Maurice and Larry followed the sideshow wagon trail measuring time by the sun's journey across the sky. Maurice's joints ached like rusty hinges from sleeping on the ground. The horses' hooves kicked up dust puffs that disappeared as fast as they formed. Larry rode past a crumpled, trampled piece of paper which Dangit stopped to sniff.

"Come on, boy, we got to keep goin'." But the dog just sat in the road and howled, so Larry doubled back and dismounted. "What you got there?" he asked, looking at the piece of paper in the dog's mouth. It took a moment for the messy handwriting to register in his mind, then he started back the way they had just come.

"What you doin'?" Maurice called out.

"Hold on a minute. It's Terry's handwritin' all right."

"What you talkin' 'bout?"

"Terry wrote a note. Somethin's wrong." Larry showed the note to Maurice.

"I figured he was with them hoboes by his free will," Maurice said. "Maybe he's just funnin' or somethin'."

Larry mounted back up. "Don't think so. Terry hates to write anything, so this must be real."

"But 'help'? What from? I kinda figured that it would be those hoboes needin' help, not the other way around."

"Find Terry, Dangit," Larry said, his expression grim. The dog took off howling after the wagon tracks.

They rode at a steady, fast pace with an uneasy feeling and found two more notes over the next three miles. Something was wrong. Maurice knew it in his bones. He didn't want to let on to Larry how worried he was, but the thought of little Terry being kidnapped by a couple of bums was frightening.

Though they figured they'd closed the gap by several hours, Maurice wondered if that was enough time to reach the wagons before Cole crossed into Arkansas. Wiping his brow, Maurice looked at Larry.

"Once they reach Arkansas, there's no tellin' which road they'll choose. But one thing's for sure, each hour that we don't catch up to 'em is an hour that they could split up and go different directions."

"Why would they do that?" Larry asked.

"No reason, except that hoboes live no-reason lives. They could jump off those wagons at any time, take the first train they see, and head for Lord-knows-where."

"And drag Terry along?"

"Maybe one has him and the other's already gone," Maurice said, trying to make sense of it all. "Anything could be happenin'."

"And if they go different directions, then what?"

"Then we'd be skunked. One might have Terry in a sack or on his back and be long gone before we knew which way they went."

Larry thought for a moment. "What if they're hurtin' him?"

"He's all right. They ain't hurt him or he wouldn't be writin' them notes."

"You sure?"

"Sure, I'm sure." Maurice sighed, not wanting to let Larry know how uncertain he really was.

"But, Mr. Springer, I can't figure out how Terry is writin' notes if one of the hoboes is holdin' him."

"The boy always finds a way to do what he wants. You know Terry."

"We gotta find him, Mr. Springer, we gotta."

"I know, son," Maurice said, looking out toward the endless woods. "The only chance we got is to take the old trail through the trees and try to ride up ahead of them."

"You think?"

"It's the only chance we got. If Terry and the hoboes hop a train, then Red may get lost in America. This is a big country, boy, and he's just a little squirt who probably don't even know how to write down where he lives." *Wish I'd packed a gun along. There's trouble comin', I can feel it in my bones.*

He floated a silent prayer, hoping it would shield him from whatever lay down the road.

33

Trapped

❖

As the wagons clomped along, Terry clung to the windows and watched the miles pass by. He felt trapped. Like an animal in a cage. Terry hated to be confined. The wagon reeked of mildewed wood and who knew what else. Looking around, he thought, *I'm headin' to someplace called Mexico with a werewolf. Don't seem real.*

Cole had brought Jo-Jo and him hard rolls and milk from a local farmer along the way, but Terry wasn't hungry. He paced two steps back and forth, creaking the boards.

"There's got to be a way to get outta this wagon," he mumbled.

Jo-Jo shook his head. "This is the punishment place. Cole uses this to keep performers in line."

"I ain't no performer."

"But you're locked in here."

"Not for long." Terry pulled at the bars. "I'm no angel, but I don't deserve bein' locked in here. No one does."

Jo-Jo cocked his head, looking at the boy. He couldn't help but smile. "You are very . . . ," he searched for the right word, ". . . cocky."

"I ain't sure what that means, but I'm gonna either break outta here or I'm gonna start screamin' like there's no tomorrow."

"Cole will beat you."

"I'll kick him if he tries." Terry shadowboxed the wall. "If'n I get my hands on Cole, I'll whup on him 'till there's nothin' left but a grease stain on the floor."

Jo-Jo giggled at Terry's antics.

Cole opened the small opening on the door and looked in. "Say, Red, maybe I'll glue red hair all over your body and tell people you're an orangutan. Make you part of my freak show."

Terry glared back. "And maybe I'll bite off your nose and tell people you picked it off."

Cole roared with laughter. Even though he was calloused to the bone, he could still appreciate the boy's spunk. "Tough little bird, ain't ya?"

"I ain't no bird, you bald-headed goose poo," Terry screamed, kicking at the door, then flip-flopping around in frustrated anger.

Cole raised his eyebrows in mild surprise at the brass in the boy. "You look like a redheaded woodpecker to me. Jo-Jo, what you think about you and this twirp doin' an act together? Werewolf Boy and Ape Boy. I think it'd be great."

Jo-Jo stayed silent, his pride long belly-down.

"Come on, dog-face, what do you think?"

Terry jumped up onto the door, clutching the window frame with tears of frustration burning his eyes. He reached out for Cole's face. "Let me outta here!"

"I'm takin' you to Mexico," Cole growled, pounding Terry's fingers.

"I don't wanna go," Terry whimpered, falling back to the floor, rubbing his hands.

"You got no choice, boy. You know too much."

"I don't know nothin'."

"You saw the bank's money, and I can't take no chances."

"*You* robbed the bank?"

Cole frowned. "I thought you knew that."

"Not for sure 'till you told me."

"Well, you know now so I can't let you go." Cole started to close the door window then paused. "Why don't you take the time to learn Spanish? Jo-Jo can teach you." He grinned, closing the hole.

Terry and Jo-Jo looked at each other as Cole's laughter echoed through the wagon.

Terry schemed until his head hurt, trying to figure a way out. Saying he had to go to the privy didn't do any good because Cole just brought him a bucket.

He thought about the car that was being pulled behind the wagon and wished he could start it up and drive away. *Pa wouldn't be mad for me doin' that.* But he knew the thought was crazy. He was desperate and worried that he'd never get home again.

Mumbling to himself, Terry paced the small space. "I gotta get out of here. I gotta get my nickel back and get on home."

"Be patient," Jo-Jo counseled, "and a way will come. Maybe in Mexico we can escape."

"Mexico! I can't wait that long! I don't even know how to find my way home from town sometimes. How am I gonna get home from Mexico?" Terry kicked the wall then turned to Jo-Jo. "Where the heck is Mexico anyway? Near China?"

"South of here. Far south. A thousand miles away."

"Oh Lordy," Terry whispered, "we go that far, and we'll be fallin' off the earth." He looked at Jo-Jo and said sadly, "I hope you really do got an angel comin' 'cause we need help."

When they stopped at noontime, Terry listened as Cole gave instructions to Roger. "I'm gonna take one of the horses and ride back to that little town we passed and get a newspaper." He wanted to see if there was any news about the bank robbery.

"Why don't you take your car?" Roger asked.

Cole shook his head. "Haven't seen a livery with a gas drum since yesterday. Don't wanna run out."

"When you gonna be back?" Roger asked.

"In a hour or so. Just keep an eye on things, and don't open Jo-Jo's door."

As Cole rode off Roger turned and saw Terry and Jo-Jo staring out at him. "Help us, please, Roger," Jo-Jo pleaded.

"Can't. You heard the man."

As the cooking fires were set to heat coffee for lunch, Terry moped in the corner, figuring his goose was cooked. Then he heard something and couldn't believe his ears.

"Ladies and gentlemen, gather 'round. My name is Railroad Jack, the man you've read about. The man the St. Louis papers call the tramp newspaperman."

Terry's eyes went wide. He popped up to the window and knew that Jack was up to something.

"Yes sir, folks, I've been hired by Mr. Cole to be part of the show so I'd like to give you all a demonstration."

Terry watched as the performers gathered around. They were a strange-looking group, giggling because they were part of the audience for the first time.

"What's your act?" little Paul shouted out.

"Yeah, you look normal to me," the three-legged man said.

"I'm who I am. If givin' money away ain't normal, then so be it, but you folks pull in close here, and I'm gonna tell you how you can each take me for a new dollar bill."

Then Terry heard the small opening on the wagon door slide back. "Psst, Red, you in there?"

It was Skeeter.

Terry hugged the old black man like there was no tomorrow. "Thanks, Skeeter."

"Don't be thankin' me yet. We still gots to cut dirt and get outta here. Come on, let's go."

Terry started through the door then turned back. "Come on, Jo-Jo. This is your chance."

The hairy-faced boy seemed frozen in place. "Where are you going?"

"We're escapin'. You're comin' too."

"I can't," Jo-Jo said. "I have nowhere else to go." He'd been with Cole for years. Suddenly the thought of leaving was frightening.

Skeeter blinked twice, then whistled softly. "Didn't see you in the corner there. Woo-wee, you need a shave."

Terry shook his head. "Werewolves don't shave. But he's my friend."

"Werewolf? For real?"

"For real," Terry nodded. He looked at Jo-Jo, who had backed against the wall away from Skeeter in fear. "You comin' or stayin'?"

Jo-Jo blinked, licking his lips rapidly. "Stayin'."

"You gotta come. Don't be stupid. This man might just be your angel."

Jo-Jo looked at Skeeter and wasn't convinced. "Cole is going to Mexico. Where my home is."

"Maybe he is, or maybe you'll just be hearin' kids make fun of you in Spanish." Jo-Jo looked down. "If you change your mind, I'm leavin' the door open. My pa will make you feel good if you want to come home with me. He's a preacher. He knows all 'bout angels."

"My home's in Mexico."

"Good luck, 'cause you'll need it," Terry said.

Jo-Jo fought back a sob, then began crying, softly at first, then shuddering tears. He wondered if he was seeing the beginning or the end of his world. The thought of running off—the thought of freedom—terrified him. Terry was the first normal boy he'd ever talked to. It had made him feel so good, so human, and now the boy was gone. Just like the Gomezes were gone. Just like his mother had let him be taken away. Old, deep pain clutched at his heart.

Skeeter peeked through the back door of the wagon. "Everyone's gathered 'round Jack. Now's our chance."

"What're we gonna do?" Terry asked. He saw Roger in the crowd. "That's Cole's man. He'll nab me for sure."

Skeeter shrugged. "Mr. Jack said to go back toward them woods over there. That he'd join us after he fleeced all the freaks for their nickels."

"Does he still gots my nickel?"

Skeeter winked. "Red, you don't let up, do ya?"

"I told you, I ain't gonna let up 'till he gives my lucky nickel back."

Skeeter hushed him. "Get ready now. We're gonna slip out."

"Hold on," Terry said, going to the front of the enclosed wagon.

"What you doin'?"

"Gotta get my pillow sack up here."

Terry poked around under the desk and found the sack.

"Come on, Red, we gotta go. Jack's gettin' winded," Skeeter whispered. There was a commotion going on outside as the performers all called out questions.

Terry turned to go, then remembered the bank's money. Reaching down under the table, he lifted up the heavy pillowcase and looked inside. There was more money than he'd ever seen in his whole life. Bundles of bills. Fifties. Hundreds. And they were all wrapped with the Bank of Mansfield's straps.

Terry took the money sack and walked back to Skeeter. "Let's go."

"What's in the sack?"

"Nothin'. Just somethin' I gotta return."

Before leaving, Terry looked in on Jo-Jo one more time. "Come with me. My pa will figure a way to get you back to Mexico."

"I can't. I'm scared."

"I'd be scared waitin' 'round for Mr. Cole to return if I was you."

"But my angel . . . I gotta trust in him."

"I'd trust my own two feet. Even angels need a little help." Terry reached out his hand. "Come on. My pa will help you."

Jo-Jo touched his hand, then grasped it. The hair tingled Terry's palm.

"Don't be a fool. Come with me," Terry repeated.

"I can't," Jo-Jo said, releasing his grasp.

"Good luck then," Terry said. Then he was gone and Jo-Jo was left alone, his heart beating fast, like a caged bird who had found the door left open.

Skeeter slipped off the side of the wagon and walked casually away from the camp. Cole's wagon was parked off by itself, which made the escape easier.

Terry stepped out and froze. The sky seemed as still as a painting, like the whole world was watching him. Reaching deep for courage, he jumped down, looked around, then saw that Roger was making a check of the camp. "He's gonna catch us for sure," he moaned, climbing up into Cole's car. He slipped under the tarp cover, praying that Roger wouldn't notice that he'd escaped.

His stomach gnawing with fear, Terry clutched the money bag, whispering, "Lord, let me get home. I'll never do nothin' bad again."

He heard footsteps. Someone was coming. His heartbeat was racing faster than a jackrabbit.

Slowly the side of the tarp was raised. Terry gulped, figuring it was Roger who was going to whip him for sure. Then two, intense eyes deep within a hood looked at him. "I'm coming with you," Jo-Jo said.

Skeeter stood in the woods waiting for Terry. Jack had finished his act and was chatting with the performers who welcomed him into the show. Roger hadn't been told about any new act, but since Jack was so smooth and put on such a good show, he figured that everything must be all right.

When Jack got to the woods, he was ready to leave. "Where's the kid?" he asked.

"Back there somewhere," Skeeter said, pointing toward the wagons. "I thought he was with you."

"He was but when I turned he was gone."

"Squirrely kid. We can't stick around forever."

"Just give him a few minutes. Maybe he's waitin' until that big man finishes his rounds." They watched Roger amble through the camp, talking with the performers, checking on the horses, mules, feed, and supplies.

"We can't stay here forever," Jo-Jo whispered.

"I know, I know," Terry snapped.

"I thought we were leaving."

"We are."

"Then why are you in here?"

"'Cause I wanted to drive the car away," Terry answered.

Jo-Jo took him seriously. "You know how to drive?"

"Sure, sure," Terry said, peeking out to see where Roger was. "If'n I just had the key we'd be hightailin' it away in style."

"The key's under here," Jo-Jo said, reaching under the steering wheel case.

Terry looked at the key and suddenly felt queasy—like he might throw up. His guts were roasting, making him dizzy. He'd gotten into this whole mess in the beginning by driving Miss Beedlebottom's car. Now, he was a runaway with a sack of stolen bank money, sitting in a car with a werewolf, with two crazy hoboes waiting for him—and he was about to steal a car. If he didn't wet his pants it would be a miracle. Everything was wrong, very wrong, and the only way to do right was to do another wrong. It was a predicament with only one right answer.

"Time to take another drive," Terry said, grabbing the key.

34

Wild Ride

❖

J ack couldn't believe his eyes. "The boy's stealin' the car," he said, watching Terry unhitch the car from the back of the wagon.

"Yup, he sure is," Skeeter grinned, admiring how fast Terry was. "He's gonna skedaddle in style."

"He's a little guttersnipe car thief is what he is. Gonna end up in jail doin' that."

"Hope he takes us with him."

"Us? I ain't gonna ride in no car that's loud 'nough to wake snakes."

"Suit yourself," Skeeter said. "But I didn't take you for such a dang old fool."

When the engine kicked into place, Terry backed up, bumping into another wagon, then he drove forward through the camp, sending the horses and performers scattering in all directions.

"Hang on!" Terry shouted, praying that he could really drive an automobile without it being tied to a pole. Jo-Jo put his head down, planning for the worst. "I might just be your shootin' star," Terry said, trying to see over the steering wheel.

Roger came running toward them, knowing that if anything happened to Cole's car he'd be held responsible. "Stop! Turn that car off!" he shouted.

"Outta the way!" Terry screamed, nearly running the man over. It wasn't easy for an eight-year-old kid to work the pedals and see over the dashboard at the same time. Roger dove under a horse, sliding through a smelly, muddy mess.

Jo-Jo clung to the door. "Watch out!" he shouted as Terry nearly ran over the three-legged man.

After two circles, Terry headed back along the road toward where he thought home was. Skeeter began waving his arms. "Wait for me. Wait for me."

"Where you goin'?" Jack asked Skeeter.

"Wherever he's goin'. Better than waitin' 'round here," Skeeter said, running after Terry.

Jack hesitated. He could not admit that he was scared to death of cars.

The camp was still in an uproar. Terry slapped Jo-Jo on the back. "Man alive, we're free!"

"Cole will come after us," Jo-Jo said flatly.

"He'll have to catch us first," Terry laughed. His feet kept slipping off the pedal, but he gripped the wheel tightly, trying to keep the car in a straight path. Then he saw Skeeter and pulled over.

"Climb in. We're goin' home."

"You know how to drive this thing?" Skeeter asked.

"Been drivin' a long time," Terry fibbed.

"Then I'm comin'." Skeeter sat behind Jo-Jo. "You got a face that would scare nine lives out of a newborn kitten, so just don't lose your hood. Folks be thinkin' we're strange 'nough, what with a redheaded crazy boy who can't barely see over the wheel drivin' a boy wearin' a hood and an ol' black man."

Skeeter saw Jack standing ten feet away. "Land's sakes, you comin'?"

Jack stood rock-solid, frozen with fear. His brain felt scrambled for the first time.

"Get in, Mr. Jack," Terry said.

Jack inched forward. Terry saw Roger and a group of performers coming toward them. "I gotta go. You comin'?"

Jack didn't say a word.

"I said, you comin'?" Terry repeated.

"I guess I am," Jack grumbled, climbing in.

Terry started forward but the car stalled. Jo-Jo looked at him through the hood. His eyes were panicked. "Start it."

"I'm tryin'," Terry said, turning the engine over and over.

"Hurry!" Jo-Jo pleaded.

The three-legged man was in the lead with Roger close behind.

Jack closed his eyes, gripping the side of the car until his knuckles cracked. "I should have never gotten into this. We got ourselves a danged spider comin' after us."

"What's wrong?" Jo-Jo whispered, gripping the door.

"We're gonna get you, Jo-Jo," Roger screamed.

Jack spit over the side. "Red, if you're just wastin' time, then let me out here so I can join the winnin' side."

The engine caught and Terry pushed the gas pedal down. Skeeter shouted, "Let 'er rip, boy!"

The car zoomed forward, but when they hit a water hole, Jo-Jo fell onto Terry, knocking the wheel out of his hands. The car spun in a circle until it was heading right back toward the sideshow posse. The three-legged man did a quick about-face and ran like there was no tomorrow.

Skeeter sat back to enjoy the ride. "Where'd you learn to drive like this?"

Terry shrugged, standing on his tiptoes, trying to make himself taller than he was. He just let out a fib naturally. "Did a lot of drivin' in St. Louie and New York."

"For real? You ain't just tellin' us a whopper?"

Terry half believed his own white lie. He wanted them to believe he knew what he was doing. That he'd been driving for a long time. He didn't want to tell them that the only driving he'd ever done was circling around a barn pole. "Yes-sir-re-bob, don't you worry. I've circled 'round a lot of places. I know what I'm doin'."

"I hope so," Jack mumbled, "'cause you don't seem to know much 'bout anythin' else."

They bounced away along the pothole-filled road. Terry turned and looked at Jack. "Now you gotta give me my nickel."

"You still after that thing? You paid to learn the secrets."

"Nope," Terry said, holding out his hand. "You said the day I got you in a car would be the day I'd get my lucky nickel back."

"That's right," Skeeter chuckled. "You sure did, Jack."

Jack frowned. "How I ever ended up in this lunatic wagon is beyond me," he said, "but you win, kid." He handed Terry his nickel.

Terry clutched it, knowing that now he was halfway home

"Now, would you hold the wheel with both hands," Jack growled, clutching the side of the car, his knuckles white with fear.

"Terry, look," Jo-Jo said. "Trouble's comin'."

Adam Cole was riding slowly toward them, too engrossed in his newspaper to notice that Terry was driving his precious car. "They think the hoboes did it. It worked. My plan worked." He laughed, congratulating himself.

The Mansfield robbery was big news and was the talk of the small town where he'd gotten the paper. The local deputy told him that the Western Union office had word that Mansfield's sheriff was leading a posse in pursuit of the hoboes, but there wasn't any local alert.

Then Cole heard the sound of a car. Looking up, always eager to admire someone else's car, he saw his own car coming straight toward him down the road.

Terry honked the horn and held up the pillow sack as they rode by. "Missin' somethin'?"

Cole was dumbfounded and suddenly felt mule-kicked stupid seeing the kid he had locked up driving past him in his own car and holding up the money he had stolen. "What the heck?" he gasped.

"Finders keepers," Terry shouted back.

Jo-Jo turned back to look at the man who had virtually owned him for almost six years. "Cole isn't moving," he said.

Jack raised his eyes. "You'd be in shock too if you saw a redheaded squirrel drivin' a couple of bums and a guy with a hood on like it was a picnic." He looked at the bag that Terry had held up. "What's in there?"

Terry shrugged. "Just some money."

"How much?"

"'Bout a million dollars I guess."

Jack fluttered his lips. "There you go, tryin' to pull a whopper on me again. The day a kid like you's got more than a nickel on him is the day I take a bath."

"Get ready for some soap," Terry grinned, tossing back the pillow sack of loot. Jack couldn't believe his eyes.

As they rounded the bend in the road, they didn't see Roger riding up to Cole with a pack of performers not too far behind.

"Sorry, Mr. Cole, but they escaped," Roger said lamely.

"I know that, you fool." Cole stared him down until Roger turned his face away. The air between them was charged and dangerous.

"Don't know how, but they escaped," Roger repeated.

"It's your fault he got the money."

"What money?"

"My money. Come on, we've got to catch 'em."

"What 'bout the freaks? You gonna just leave 'em?"

Cole saw them gathered a quarter mile back. "Tell them to wait by the wagons. We'll be back by dark. Grab yourself one of my Arkansas toothpicks and some pistols. Hurry!"

Within minutes Roger was riding after Terry wearing a brace of pistols stuck in his belt with a huge bowie knife strapped against his leg.

Terry honked and waved to farmers and riders as if it were just a day in the park. He was all over the road, but luckily there wasn't much traffic. Jack was the world's worst backseat driver, so Terry did his best to bug him by driving with one hand. Once, when they were going down a little ridge, he even sat back on the seat and drove the car with his feet.

"You're gonna get us killed," Jack complained.

"Not until you've had a bath, Mr. Stinkbug."

Terry slowed to let an old sow amble across the road, then floored the accelerator. When the car backfired, an old woman shouted, "Get a horse."

"She's just jealous," Terry laughed.

Jack was not happy. No self-respecting hobo would let a kid drive him around like a wet nurse. "Let me out right here," he demanded.

"Why?" Skeeter asked.

"Just drop me off at the nearest railroad tracks, and I'll hitch a real ride."

"Nope," Terry said, having the time of his life.

"Nope?"

"Not until after you've had a bath. I'm tired of hangin' 'round a man who smells like old cheese."

"That's a fine lot of thanks I get for all I learned you."

"You're welcome," Terry grinned, winking at Jo-Jo.

Jack grumbled, "Think I spent all my life learnin' the ways of the road."

"So?" Terry asked.

"So I sure know better than ridin' in a car with a kid and Mr. Hairy up there." Jo-Jo turned. "No offense, but you are kinda hairy and this ain't my idea of fun."

"Guess you need some cheerin' up." Terry smiled and began whistling "Yankee Doodle." Jack's moans made them all laugh.

Crossed Paths

❖

When the sheriff and his men met up with Maurice and Larry, they filled each other in on what they knew and about the note that Dangit had found. It was like a jigsaw puzzle that was now missing only three pieces. Terry, the money, and the bank robber.

Sheriff Peterson asked, "Maurice, who do you think took the money?"

"I ain't done no thinkin' 'bout that. We've been lookin' for the boy."

"You think he's tied in with it somehow?"

"No, you read the notes."

"Maybe it's a trick."

Larry frowned, cocking his head. "You think my brother robbed the bank?"

"No, but you know how kids can be. Maybe he fell in with some bad men and just left town. You know, for the adventure."

"Not Terry," Larry said defensively. He looked over at Maurice who was giving him one of those don't-be-too-sure looks.

"Well," the sheriff said, straightening his hat, "the one thing I know is that robbin' a bank is a hangin' offense."

"They wouldn't hang a kid . . . would they?" Maurice wondered, now worried that Terry really was mixed up in the robbery somehow.

"No, but they'll send him to jail if he's mixed up in this."

The thought of Terry sitting in jail with a long white beard dumbfounded Larry. "You can't put a kid in jail."

"They can and they do," Sheriff Peterson answered.

The sheriff and his men headed south along the ridge trail, following the old hunter's trail which they figured would save time. Maurice wanted to keep to the main road, but he knew he had to make speed if he was going to catch Terry. He watched the sheriff and his men ride away until they were just dust balls on the horizon. "You think your brother's a bank robber?" he asked Larry.

"Terry's done a lot of crazy things, but he ain't never robbed a bank."

"First time for everything," Maurice said, wondering as they rode back along the road if they were on the trail of a miniature Jesse James. Then he came to his senses and figured that Terry had been kidnapped. That he had had no choice but to go along with the hoboes.

When they met up with a circuit-riding preacher who knew the local area, he told them to follow an old wagon path through the hills which he said was a short cut. "It merges up ahead before the Crossroads Store."

Dangit was the first to find it.

Cole and Roger rode their horses hard. Determined to use his pistol to save his Mexican dream, Cole knew it was an all or nothing race against time. If Terry got back to Mansfield, then Cole's plan was ruined. He could ride back to his wagons now, and hightail it toward Mexico, but he doubted he'd make the Texas border before he was caught. You couldn't just race a dozen wagons filled with freaks unnoticed through the countryside. Every wagon was colorfully designed to attract attention. But now attention was the last thing Cole wanted if he was going to escape the law—and Stein.

He touched his pistol, wondering if he would have the guts to use it if the chips were down. "Hope it don't come to that," he whispered.

Railroad Jack sat with the money bag on his lap. He couldn't believe it. There was more money in his hands than he'd ever seen in his life. Peeking into the bag again, he calculated that he'd have to answer about ten million questions to earn enough nickels to equal what he was holding.

"What you gonna do with the money? Split it up?" he asked Terry. Terry made a face. "Split it up?"

"Yeah, divvy it up the hobo way. Just between us buddies "

"Nope," Terry said flatly, "I'm takin' it back."

"Back? You mean to tell me you're gonna give back all this money? Thought you were runnin' away."

"I'm goin' home. That's where I wanna be."

"You sure now?" Jack asked, pressing the boy.

"I know I shouldn't have left," Terry admitted.

"You know what you did was wrong, don't you?"

"Yup. I know that what you told me is true. That there's no place like home."

"Amen," whispered Skeeter.

From the ridge above the road, Cole pointed down. "There they are. Get your pistol out and follow me."

36

Candy Break

❖

After a few miles, Terry was driving like a pro. He knew nothing about the car needing gas or what to do if he got a flat tire; all he knew was that if he kept the car in the middle of the road and held the wheel tight, he'd get back to Mansfield if he just kept following the signs.

Along the way though, something was on his mind. Something that he really needed. Terry was thinking about candy and the fact that the bank probably wouldn't miss a dollar from the bag. "Least they could do is reward me with a candy dollar," he decided, knowing he'd make history of the first bag of candy he got his hands on.

Then he saw the Crossroads Store up ahead and made his decision. He had no idea that Cole and Roger were making their way down the ridge or that Maurice and his brother were watering their horses in the barn behind the store.

"Anybody hungry?" he asked.

"You got food?" Skeeter asked.

"You been hoardin' on us, Red?" Jack grumbled.

"Nope, there's a store up ahead. Thought we'd get us some grub."

While Jack and Skeeter talked about the pickles and crackers they were going to get, Terry envisioned jars of candy of every color and taste imaginable.

The string-bean-looking store owner was standing out front in an apron, waving them to come in. His crooked mouth was split into a grin as he figured that anyone driving a car in those parts had to be rich.

"Who's got money?" Jack wondered aloud.

"We got a bagful," Terry exclaimed, so excited thinking about the candy that he almost drove off the road.

"Thought you were takin' the bank's money back," Jack said, mimicking Terry's voice.

Terry answered, "We can spend a few bucks to keep ourselves alive."

"If you can just pretty-as-you-please take that money, then how 'bout we just buy the store, and you leave me and Skeeter here to run it?"

"Sounds fine by me." Skeeter smiled.

"Can't do that," Terry said, concentrating on stopping the car before he hit the store.

The man in the front of the store stopped waving when Terry didn't slow down. He realized that Terry was heading directly toward the side of the store.

"You better slow down," Jo-Jo cautioned.

The store owner was in a panic, jumping up and down, signaling for them to stop.

"I'm tryin' to but the brakes ain't workin'," Terry shouted.

"Oh Lordy," Skeeter whispered as they got closer to the front window of the store.

"Pump the brake pedal," Jo-Jo advised. "Maybe it's stuck."

That did the trick and Terry was able to bring the car to a halt alongside the building.

The store owner was angry. "You tryin' to joke on me?"

"Nope. Just had brake trouble."

"You're just a kid!" the store owner exclaimed. "And you're just bums," he added when he saw Jack and Skeeter.

"I beg your pardon," Jack said indignantly.

"We're hoboes," Skeeter said, as if that made a difference.

"And what's under there?" he asked, pointing to Jo-Jo's hood.

Terry shrugged. "He's got a cold. Doctor said to keep his face covered so it won't spread."

"You better travel on. Only folks with money allowed in here," the store owner said, looking them over carefully.

"We got money," Terry said.

"You'd better, or I'll run you out," the store owner huffed, walking back inside.

"Do we got money," Terry mumbled. He reached into the bag and handed each one a buck.

"One measly dollar," Jack fumed.

"That's enough to get a bite," Terry argued.

"Look," Skeeter said, pointing to the poster on the front of the store. Someone had put up a hand-drawn announcement about the bank robbery and the reward being offered.

"They're offerin' a thousand bucks for bringin' either the money back or the robbers." Terry whistled.

"Then you're gonna be rich," Skeeter said. "What you gonna do with all that money?"

"Gonna do somethin' I really wanna do. Like maybe buy a candy store or somethin'."

Suddenly the wood burst apart on the wall above their heads. "Someone's shootin' at us!" Jack shouted. Two men were riding hard toward them with pistols drawn.

Maurice heard the shots and ruckus and came running out from the barn behind the Crossroads Store where he and Larry had been watering their horses. He saw two riders coming down the hill fast.

"What's goin' on?" Larry called out.

"Trouble's comin', that's all I know."

Dangit ran out toward the front just as Maurice recognized it was Cole firing the gun. "Lord I wish I'da brought a gun," Maurice moaned. He knew the man wasn't bringing any free tickets this time.

Terry started up the car. "Come on, let's go!" He drove forward.

Roger stood up in his stirrups to throw his knife, but Terry drove straight toward him. "Don't hit me," Roger shouted, riding his horse out of the way.

"Get us outta here!" Skeeter shouted, standing up in the seat, sweat streaming from his pores.

"Get down," Jack said, pulling at his friend as another bullet whizzed by them.

Cole raised his pistol and fired as Terry drove under a low-hanging branch. Skeeter thumped backward in the seat as the owner of the store came running outside.

"He's hit!" Jack shouted.

Terry drove forward just missing the store owner but managing to knock down a rack of beef jerky. "Hold on!" he screamed, steering past a squealing pig. He didn't see his brother waving from the side of the store or realize that the barking dog was Dangit.

"Get a doctor!" Jack pleaded, cradling Skeeter's head in his lap. He looked around, wondering where all the blood was. "Don't want to lose my travelin' buddy."

Everything was helter-skelter. It was a miracle that Terry missed the store, the water tank, and the big tree. But he kept the gas pedal floored as another bullet whizzed by them.

Jack looked at his friend. "Skeeter, wake up, show me where you were shot." Slowly he lifted up Skeeter's shirt to see if there was a wet mess from the bullet. But there wasn't anything. Not one drop of blood.

The old black man opened his eyes and blinked. "Didn't see the branch," he moaned, rubbing the goose-egg-sized lump on the back of his head.

Maurice yelled to Terry but Terry didn't hear him. Dangit was busy eating up the beef jerky scattered all over the ground before the store owner could stop him.

"Larry, come on, we got to help your brother," Maurice yelled.

"He's drivin' a car," Larry said in amazement. "Pa's gonna be mad."

"Then don't tell him. Now get saddled up while I settle with the store owner for Dangit's lunch."

Cole rode in the dust trail behind the car, waving for Roger to catch up. There was ice in his blood. His temples throbbed. He knew that if he didn't catch Terry and his sidekicks the money would be gone forever, and the law would soon be on his tail.

Can't let him get away. Can't let him live to tell what he knows. He looked at Roger, then back at the car up ahead. *Might have to just ride off alone with the money once things are taken care of.*

❖ ❖ ❖

Terry knew he had to do something quickly, or he'd never get a chance to spend that thousand-dollar reward on candy. Desperate to escape, he watched the road, looking for a place to pull over or a house to drive behind.

"You know where you're goin'?" Jo-Jo asked, holding tightly to the side.

"Nope. Just know I gotta *keep* goin'."

"Pull over and let me out," Jack shouted. "Think I'm gonna get sick."

"Puke over the side," Terry said, "'cause I ain't stoppin' yet."

As they flew over the next ridge, barely touching the road, Terry saw an old trail splitting off to the left and took it.

"What're you doin'?" Jack shouted as the tree branches closed in.

"Gotta find a place to hide."

The trail opened up to a wagon's width. "You think your Danny Boone or somethin'?" Jack asked, wiping a spiderweb off his face.

"Hush. We gotta hide."

Terry pulled the car into the bushes and shut off the engine. They watched as Cole and Roger raced past their hiding place up the road.

"How long we gonna sit here, Red?" Jack asked.

"As long as we got to."

"But now we're trapped. They're ahead of us and no tellin' what kind of freaks are comin' behind us."

Then they heard someone coming through he woods on the trail. Terry froze, wondering if he should start up the car.

"Mr. Gomez!" Jo-Jo shouted, jumping out of the car.

37

Wagon South

❖

Gomez pulled his wagon to a halt. "Jo-Jo," he exclaimed. "What are you doing here?"

In a moment there was a teary-eyed reunion in Spanish. Terry wondered what they were saying but was just plain happy for Jo-Jo's sake. They were making so much racket that he hoped that Cole hadn't doubled back because he'd for sure hear them.

Gomez lifted Jo-Jo's hood off and appeared to ask him a serious question. Jo-Jo nodded, looking at the other family members, saying, "Si, si, si," over and over. Jo-Jo turned to Terry and said proudly, his eyes glistening, "They want to take me home with them to Mexico. Said I'll never have to wear the hood again."

"They did?"

Jo-Jo nodded. "To their home. To be part of their family."

"That's great," Terry smiled.

"Then I should go with them?"

"Go," Terry said.

Jo-Jo ran back over to hug Mrs. Gomez. Terry whispered, "Guess some angels ride in wagons."

"Those are just plain, good people. Salt of the earth," Jack said.

Jo-Jo walked over to Terry and hugged him. "You will always be my friend for what you did."

"Didn't do nothin' 'cept learn somethin' 'bout you."

Jo-Jo tried to blink back tears but couldn't. "You set me free," he whispered. Then he turned to Skeeter and Jack. "And you both did too. You let me escape."

"Just helped you escape," Skeeter said, trying to correct the boy.

"No, you let me escape. I had to want to go."

"You're gonna need some money," Terry said, reaching into the pillow sack.

Jo-Jo stopped him. "No. Take the money back to your bank and go home. That is what's right."

Terry thought for a moment, then reached into his pocket and pulled out his lucky nickel. "I want you to have this."

Jo-Jo shook his head. "No, I can't. That's your special nickel. The one that your father won for you."

"My pa would want you to have it," Terry said, pushing it into the boy's hairy hand."

Jo-Jo held it up between two fingers. "But it's yours."

"My pa says that if my heart was in the right place that this nickel would take me to faraway places."

"Your heart's in the right place," Jo-Jo whispered.

"Then you take the nickel with you to Mexico. That's about as far away as the moon."

Mr. Gomez said they'd better hurry. If Cole found them, they knew he'd take Jo-Jo back to the sideshow.

"Well, good-bye," Terry said softly, blinking back a tear.

"I will pray for you," Jo-Jo said as he climbed into the wagon.

"You got any money?" Terry asked Mr. Gomez.

"We have twelve dollars. That's enough."

Terry reached into the bag and pulled out a handful of banded bills. "How much of this makes a thousand?" he asked Jack.

"Count it yourself."

"I can't count that high."

Jack took two five-hundred-dollar bands and held them up. "Here's a thousand."

Terry put the rest of the money back in the sack and turned to Mr. Gomez.

Gomez stared at the money. He hesitated to touch it. "I can't take your money."

Terry shrugged, putting the money into his hands. "You just take good care of Jo-Jo and make sure my nickel makes it to Mexico."

"I'll miss you," Jo-Jo called out from the wagon.

"Me too. Just rub that nickel for luck and you'll be all right."

As the Mexican family rode off, Jo-Jo peeked out from under the blankets where he was hiding. "I'm going home with my new family," he whispered, hoping it wasn't a dream.

"Your angel told me that your home is with us now," Mrs. Gomez said, hugging the boy. "Now stay under the blanket until we know you're safe."

Jo-Jo closed his eyes and went to sleep, rubbing Terry's lucky nickel between his fingers, wondering if angels had red hair.

Showdown

❖

Ain't it about time we got goin'?" Jack asked, worried that they were pressing their luck by waiting around.

Terry was still looking down the trail, but the Gomez wagon was long out of sight. "I guess."

Jack could smell trouble, and butterflies of fear were taking flight in his stomach. "It won't take long for that Mr. Cole to figure out that we tricked him, and he'll come doublin' back to look for our tracks."

Terry looked around. "Guess you're right."

Jack shook his head. "Kinda worries me that the kid drivin' the car don't know nothin' better than guesses."

Skeeter was worried too and could feel the sweat running down from under his arms. "We ought to get while the gettin's good. No sense lookin' for trouble to find us. Ain't that right, Red?"

Before Terry could answer, they all heard the crack of the brush behind them.

"Hands up!" Cole shouted, stepping out from the bushes with a pistol in his hand. Roger appeared from the other side.

Jack mumbled, "We've done stepped into it now."

"I said, hands up!" Cole said angrily.

"Do what the man says," mumbled Skeeter, raising his arms, seeing the hair-trigger danger in Cole's eyes.

"We ain't done nothin'," Terry said.

"Just stole my car, my money, and my freak." Cole looked around. "Where's Jo-Jo?"

Jack said, "He ran off into the woods."

"He what?" Cole shouted, looking around.

Jack chuckled. "Said he wanted to join up with a wolf pack."

"Wolf pack? You're lyin'."

"You stinkin' robber," Terry said, bristling that the man had found them.

"I'm sick of your big mouth, little runt," Cole said, pointing the gun at Terry's face. "Now give me the money and get away from my car."

Terry handed him the pillow sack.

"Roger, you tie these three up. We're gonna get ourselves a reward."

"Reward?" Skeeter said. "But it's you who done robbed the bank."

"You robbed the bank? Is that why you're going to Mexico?" Roger asked.

Cole shrugged. "Did what I had to do. There's a piece in it for you."

"You gonna kill us?" Jack asked.

Cole nodded.

"Even little Red?" Skeeter asked quietly.

Cole cleared his throat. "Accidents happen. Law will understand and give me the reward." He held up the sack. "They'll never know what happened to the bank's money. I'll be in Mexico before they ever suspect me."

The sheriff pushed his horse hard along the road. The hysterical store owner said there had been a gun battle between a man and a car full of hoboes. The sheriff was certain it had something to do with the stolen money and the two hoboes he was searching for.

"Just keep followin' the tire tracks," he called out to his men.

Maurice watched from the bushes as Cole threatened Terry. He and Larry had kept their distance as they followed Cole, figuring that the man would lead them to Terry. Dangit had barely been able to keep up with his stomach full of jerky, and now Maurice held tightly to Dangit's collar. The story was starting to come together, and when Maurice heard what Cole said, it all made sense.

Now, if he could just keep Cole from shooting someone, things would work out just fine. But that was a big "if" from the way Cole was waving his gun around.

"What're we gonna do?" Larry asked. "Sic Dangit on 'em?"

Dangit had rolled onto his back with his feet in the air. "Not likely," Maurice answered. "Dog looks like a stuffed tick."

"Then what are we gonna do?" Larry worried.

Maurice thought for a moment, then whispered, "You go on 'round the other side and when I say the word *posse,* you start racin' 'round, rattlin' the bushes, makin' 'nough noise to sound like an army."

"But there's only two of us," Larry protested.

"And there's two of them. You just go on and do as I say." Larry crept off, hoping for the best.

Maurice knew that their odds weren't very good. *Now, what am I gonna say to that crazy man?* he wondered as he looked through the bushes at Cole with his loaded gun.

Cole lined his three prisoners up against the bushes. "Roger, tie the hoboes' hands."

"What 'bout the kid?" Roger asked, his ropy, thick muscles tensed for a fight.

Cole looked at the boy who had caused him so much trouble. "Tie him up too until I figure out what kind of accident he's gonna have."

"You doin' this to us for money?" Skeeter asked in amazement.

"Is there any other reason to waste two good bullets on hoboes?"

"How 'bout you ask me a question," Jack suggested.

"Don't listen to him, Mr. Cole," Roger urged.

"I've heard his act," Cole chuckled.

Jack started right in. "I was just sayin' before I was interrupted that if I can't answer your question, you can shoot me. But if I do, then you let us go and keep the money."

"Not a bad deal," Cole said, pretending to consider it.

"Best deal in town," Jack nodded, thinking they had a chance.

"But I'd rather turkey shoot you two hoboes and let the kid have an accident. That way I keep the money and no one knows."

"He'll know," Skeeter said, pointing up.

"And I'll deal with Him when I get there."

Terry wondered if it was too late for prayers. He started thinking about all the church words he knew. *Hope God's not got His ears turned off.*

He nearly dropped to his knees as Maurice stepped out from the bushes. "Mr. Springer!"

Maurice winked. "Give it up, boys. We got you covered."

Cole spun around, thinking it was the law. Then he saw that it was the black farmer from Mansfield and he was unarmed. "This ain't no hootenanny, farmer. You ain't got no business here," he said coldly.

"I said to give it up, we got you covered," Maurice said, trying to look stern.

"You ain't got anybody covered. You ain't even armed." Cole laughed.

"I mean business," Maurice said, trying to sound angry.

"You're probably just lookin' for more free tickets. Roger, tie him up too. He probably just came to steal back my bank money." He looked at Maurice and fired a shot in the air. "You just bought yourself a one-way ticket to your Maker," he said.

Maurice's eyebrows touched his hairline. "The sheriff's got a posse out there," he said loudly, waving his hand all around, trying to act brave, expecting Larry to respond. There was only silence.

"Posse, eh?" Cole chuckled. "I think you're all alone." He fired off another shot.

"Believe me, we've got a *posse* out there," Maurice said more loudly.

Larry finally heard the word and began making noises, wiggling the bushes, grunting, making man sounds. Cole and Roger looked around.

Maurice said smugly, "Now you just drop your guns and turn yourselves in all peaceful like."

Cole grabbed the money sack and pulled Terry to his side. "I'm taking the kid and the money."

"No you ain't," Maurice said, inching forward.

As Cole dragged Terry toward his horse, the boy kicked and screamed, "You ain't takin' me nowhere!" Wiggling to arm's length, he managed to kick Cole as hard as he could, smack-dab in the shins.

Cole hopped up and down on one foot. "Dangit! That hurts!"

Dangit opened his eyes and sat up. He'd heard his name misused and went racing out into the clearing and latched onto the cuff of Cole's pant leg, spinning the man in circles, trying to rip his cuff off.

"Let go!" Cole screamed, dropping the pistol.

Maurice picked it up. "Now I got you covered."

Cole's courage melted when he faced his own gun.

Maurice looked over at Roger and said, "Drop your gun. Now."

"I didn't do nothin'," Roger said, lowering his pistol.

"That's what I think too. But if you don't drop your gun the sheriff's gonna arrest you for bank robbin'."

"I'll be the judge of that," Sheriff Peterson said, stepping out from the bushes.

39

Reunion

❖

Though Mr. Givens, the bank manager, was surprised that Terry had taken his reward in advance, he was ecstatic to get the rest of the money back. The bank was saved. It wouldn't go under.

Railroad Jack and Skeeter got some of the credit for bringing the money back, and the bank offered to put them up in the hotel and feed them for a week. The hotel agreed on the condition that they take hot, soapy baths before they slept in the beds. Jack reluctantly agreed at Skeeter's prodding.

The sheriff locked Cole and Roger up and had his posse members round up the sideshow wagons to return them to Stein, who said he'd offer a new and better deal to any of the performers who would stay.

Terry rode quietly behind Maurice on the horse toward home. "What am I gonna say to Pa?" he asked.

"Just let your heart talk. Knowin' where you been helps you set your course on where you wanna go."

"But I runned away and I gave away my lucky nickel." Terry explained how he had given the nickel to Jo-Jo and reward money to Mr. Gomez. "Your pa's gonna understand. Don't take a preacherman to understand why you did what you did."

"And I stole a car."

"No need to start tellin' your pa all that when you first see him. Give him a chance to welcome you back 'fore you start tellin' him 'bout takin' another car."

"Yeah," Larry said, having heard the conversation, "just give Pa a big ol' hug. He'll do the rest."

When they rode up to the house Terry saw his father standing on the porch, watching them as they drew closer. Sherry stood with the door open, wondering what was going to happen.

"There's Pa," Terry whispered, going over in his mind everything he'd done. The bad things. The fibs. The running away. He didn't even want to think about stealing the pie, the car, and the sack of money.

"Found somebody you've been lookin' for," Maurice said to Rev. Youngun as he dismounted.

Terry stayed on the horse, looking small and scared. His father slowly stepped down from the porch without saying a word, his heart swelling with relieved happiness. Lifting Terry from the horse he hugged him and whispered, "I'm glad you're home, son."

"There's no place like home," Terry sobbed, hugging his father like there was no tomorrow and wishing he could erase the past few days.

Maurice stood back, wiping his own tears. Larry took Sherry by the hand and walked her inside, wiping his wet eyes. It was Terry's time to be alone with their father.

"But I gave away your nickel, the lucky nickel you won me," Terry whispered, nestling his face into his father's shoulder.

"I'll win you another. You have my promise on that. Now let's go toss the ball and have some fun together," Rev. Youngun said.

A week later Railroad Jack and Skeeter came by before they left town. Terry barely recognized them in their new store-bought clothes and smelling like flowers.

"Gonna miss you, kid," Jack said.

"Gonna miss you too, Mr. Jack. And you too, Skeeter," Terry said, hugging both men together. He wanted to cry. "And you finally got your bath."

Skeeter laughed. "He fought like a cat in a tub."

"Wasn't as bad as I feared," Jack grinned.

"And he smells better than I expected," Skeeter laughed.

"Thanks for all the lessons," Terry said, managing to smile.

Jack ruffled Terry's hair. "Red, you've got your whole life ahead of you while I'm kinda windin' mine down. Whatever you do, the only lesson I want you to remember is that you've got your own road in life. Don't be thinkin' that some other fellow's road is a better way to go."

Terry nodded, blinking back tears.

Skeeter leaned over and gave him a hug. "We'll see you 'round if we hitch back through this town."

"I'll miss you both," Terry said again.

"Just remember the hobo lessons I taught you," Jack said, doing a little hobo wiggle-walk.

"I won't forget." Terry smiled.

Jack knelt down and put his arm on Terry's shoulder. "Always remember, kid, there's no place better than your own home."

"I know that now." Terry nodded as the tears streamed down his cheeks. They hugged once more and said good-bye. Terry could hardly speak and just stood there, his small hand waving slowly up and down. The sunlight shimmered in his eyes as he watched and waved until he couldn't see them anymore.

40

Common Bond

❖

When it came time for the Fall county fair, Rev. Youngun and Terry were the first in line at the ring toss booth. Terry closed his eyes with each pitch of the ring, and finally, after six tries, his father won him another lucky nickel.

Kneeling down, Rev. Youngun put the nickel into his son's hand. "This one is my promise to you that I'll always try to make time for you," Rev. Youngun said, hugging his son.

"And I promise to try and be better," Terry smiled.

Taking Terry by the hand, Rev. Youngun asked, "You want to see the sideshow?"

"No, Pa. Don't seem right laughin' at people like that."

Walking along with his father, having the kind of time he'd wished for, Terry rubbed his new nickel with all his might. "Hope Jo-Jo's all right," he whispered.

Terry had told his father all about Jo-Jo, about the angel star he had wished for and how he gave Jo-Jo the lucky nickel and Mr. Gomez the reward money. Though Rev. Youngun could have used the money to help the family, he couldn't fault Terry for having his heart in the right place.

"You think Jo-Jo made it to Mexico, Pa?"

"I'm sure he did. You did a good thing, giving him your nickel. I told you it would take you to faraway places."

Terry nodded, looking away, blinking back tears. "And it did. I feel a little piece of me went with Jo-Jo, wherever he is."

Rev. Youngun picked his son up and carried him. "It did, son, it did. Your heart's wherever that boy is now."

"He's in Mexico. I just know it, Pa," Terry whispered, looking off into the distance.

In his heart Terry knew that Jo-Jo had made it to Mexico with his new family. He could feel it as he rubbed the new nickel, and he was right. Somewhere down in Mexico, at that very moment, Jo-Jo was rubbing his lucky nickel, thinking about the redheaded boy who had changed his life. The boy he called his redheaded angel.

Two boys from two worlds linked together by the common bond of simple friendship. A thousand miles apart, both thinking about each other, knowing there was no place like home. Which just goes to show that five cents can take you a long way if your heart's in the right place.

Turn the page
for an excerpt from

Thomas L. Tedrow's

The Legend of the
Missouri Mud Monster

Book Four
Younguns series

Larry looked toward Bedal's store, hoping his sister wouldn't come out until the Dark Hats had passed.

Terry saw the talking crow who lived in their barn circling overhead. "Edgar Allan Crow thinks it's a funeral," he said.

Larry said, "Hope he don't . . ." then stopped as the crow dive-bombed down, screeching, "Rise and shine!" Mrs. Robison swatted at the bird as the crow grabbed at her hat. Her husband dropped the reins, trying to help his screaming wife. The crow swooped over the horses, spooking them. In a blink of an eye, they bolted down the dusty street, scattering the Saturday shoppers. The Robisons' mail flew out of the back of the wagon, scattering down the street.

Sherry thanked Mr. Bedal for giving her the extra gumdrops. "Bet you gave me a whole extra half pound," she grinned.

"Close to a pound." The storekeeper winked.

Maurice slipped him a nickel. "That's for the extra."

"You don't have to do that," Mr. Bedal said.

"Then leave it as an account, 'case one of them Youngun kids comes back broke."

"You mean like Terry?" Mr. Bedal laughed.

Maurice nodded. "Kinda had him in mind. He's got a sweet tooth bigger'n you can imagine."

"Good-bye, Mr. and Mrs. Springer," Sherry said, skipping out into the middle of the street. She stopped to take out a red gum ball.

Terry's eyes went wide when he saw his sister standing in the path of the Dark Hats' runaway wagon. "Move, Sherry!" he screamed, and took off running to help her.

Sherry looked up and saw the wagon coming. "It's the Dark Hats," she whispered, feeling her heart jump.

"Get outta the way!" Larry shouted, but his sister stood frozen, like a deer caught in a hunter's jacklights. Larry ran toward the wagon and grabbed at the reins, hoping to stop it but was swept off his feet as his wrists tangled in the reins. A couple of men ran to help, but the horses were moving too fast, dragging Larry down the street.

Sherry stood petrified, her long, bony little-girl legs locked straight, the candy bag clutched in her hand. "Dark Hats!" she whispered.

Terry raced to save the sister he loved to torment, but the wagon was gaining on him. *Gotta save her,* he told himself over and over.

Every second counted.

The Robisons bounced helplessly. The reins were out of John's reach. Sarah had fallen into the back of the wagon on top of the feed sacks. John shouted for the horses to stop, but they raced on, a galloping wagon of death dragging Larry down the street straight toward Sherry.

Maurice and Eulla Mae came out of Bedal's General Store. She grabbed his arm. "Maurice, look. Larry's caught in the reins."

"Oh, Lord," he whispered and dropped the groceries he was holding. "Don't let go!" he shouted to Larry, as he took off. He knew that if Larry dropped the reins, he'd be trampled by the team of horses.

Eulla Mae then saw Sherry and ran toward her. "Move, girl! Move outta the way!" she shouted.

"It's the Dark Hats," Sherry whispered, over and over, thinking her nightmares had come to take her to the orphanage.

Maurice cut directly in front of the approaching team, waving his jacket back and forth. "Whoa, stop there, ease up." It was a matter of great nerve because if the horses didn't stop, Maurice himself would have been trampled. Eulla Mae closed her eyes. The horses didn't slow down.

"Stop, fools!" Maurice shouted.

Terry tackled Sherry, and they rolled into the muddy edge of the wooden sidewalk just as Maurice brought the wagon to a halt.

"You all right?" Terry whispered.

"Don't let the Dark Hats get me" Sherry pleaded.

"I won't."

"Is Pa dead?"

"No. You just had a fright. Now stand up 'fore you ruin your dress." He looked at the bag of candy in her hand. "Here, let me carry that for you. Too heavy for a girl to be foolin' with." Sherry was too shaken up to think straight and handed him the bag.

Eulla Mae picked Sherry up. "Girl, you coulda gotten killed."

"It's the Dark Hats," Sherry said, snuggling against Eulla Mae's shoulder.

Eulla Mae wiped the dust from the girl's face. Her dark chocolate skin contrasted against Sherry's pale, ashen face. "God was with you today," she said soothingly. A warm wind flapped the ruffles of her blouse.

Maurice knelt down beside Larry. "You all right?" he asked, dusting Larry's shirt off.

"Thought I was a goner."

"Your daddy's gonna be mad 'bout this," Maurice sighed, looking at the long tear in the seams.

"Don't need to worry that poor man none," Eulla Mae said, "I'll sew that up for you. Just thank the Lord you're alive. Praise God," she said with fervor. Sherry snuggled deep into her arms.

"I don't know what in the sam hill started it all, but that was a brave thing to do," Sheriff Peterson said loudly, pointing to Terry. "Saw it all from down the street but couldn't do nothin'." He pushed the holstered Navy Colt pistol back over on his side.

Terry came up smiling, his mouth stuffed with chewy gumdrops. "Guessyou'dcallmeahero,huh?"

"What'd you say?"

"I'mahero,huh?" he mumbled, licking the sugar off his fingers.

"What's in your mouth?" Maurice asked. But before Terry could answer, he continued, "I saw you racin' to save your sister. Bravest thing I ever saw you done."

Terry swallowed the lump in his mouth. "Didn't want nothin' to happen to her. Gotta love your sister the Lord says."

Sherry suddenly came to her senses. "Where's my candy?"

"Guess you were worried 'bout the bag of sweets too," Maurice laughed.

"Who gots my candy?" Sherry asked, looking around.

"Did you drop it?" Eulla Mae asked.

Terry tossed the bag to his brother. "Larry's got it."

Sherry squirmed down and grabbed it. "He ate half my gumdrops!" Then she saw the Dark Hats get down from the wagon. She backed away, eyes wide. "That's the woman I had bad dreams about," she whispered, grabbing on to Eulla Mae's legs.

About the Author

❖

Thomas L. Tedrow is a best-selling author, screenwriter, and film producer. He prides himself on writing stories that families can read together and pass on to friends. He is the author of the best-selling eight-book series The Days of Laura Ingalls Wilder, the eight-book series The Younguns, and such new classics as *Dorothy—Return to Oz, Grizzly Adams & Kodiak Jack,* and other books and stories. Tedrow lives with his wife, Carla, and their four children in Winter Park, Florida.

Don't miss any of the exciting adventures of

THE
YOUNGUNS

Keep up with the kids who can't seem
to stay out of trouble.
Larry, Terry, and Sherry Youngun
get into mischief like bees into honey
yet cherish honesty, compassion,
courage, and kindness.